DANGER IN PARADISE

KATIE REUS

*****

Katie Reus
Copyright © 2011 by Katie Reus
ISBN-13: 978-1492177869
ISBN-10: 1492177865

Praise for the novels of Katie Reus

Alpha Instinct is a wild, hot ride for readers. The story grabs you and doesn't let go. —*New York Times* bestselling author, Cynthia Eden

"Sinful, Sexy, Suspense... Katie Reus pulls you in and never lets go." —*USA Today* bestselling author, Laura Wright

"His Secret Past was an action packed page turner." — Night Owl Reviews

"...No One to Trust was a fast-paced, steamy romantic suspense with quite a bit of emotional depth. I would recommend it to any fan of the genre." —RR&H Novel Thoughts & Book Talk

"I couldn't put this book down. This was the whole package for me and I can't wait to read more of this author's books. This is definitely a book I will read again!" —Secrets of a Book Lover

"Explosive danger and enough sexual tension to set the pages on fire . . . fabulous!" —*New York Times* bestselling author, Alexandra Ivy

"Sexy alphas, kick-ass heroines, and twisted villains will keep you turning the pages . . . a winner." —Caridad Piñeiro, *New York Times* bestselling author

"Nonstop action, a solid plot, good pacing and riveting suspense..." —*RT Book Reviews (4.5 Stars)*

Dedication

For Denica. Thank you for all that you do.

Chapter 1

Hope Jennings nearly fell out of bed at the shrill ringing that sliced through her dreamless sleep. She blinked as she tried to focus on the digital clock on her nightstand. *Four in the morning.*

Struggling to see, she picked up her phone. "Hello?" she rasped out. Eyes closed, she fell back against the pillow.

"Your time is coming bitch," a voice said softly. Too softly to tell if it was a man or woman.

Oh Lord, another prank caller. She should have turned off her ringer. "Don't you have anything better to do than bother people this late?" She rolled over, ready to hang up, when the voice stopped her.

"You're going to pay for what you did to my face." Still soft, there was a deadly edge to that voice now.

As if she'd received a shot of adrenaline straight to her chest, her heart stuttered and she bolted straight up. She pushed the comforter off.

"That got your attention, didn't it?"

"What do you want?" The question came out hoarse and scratchy.

"I want you dead."

"That's mighty tough talk over the phone." She couldn't believe she managed to find her voice when all

1

she wanted to do was hang up and pretend this call wasn't happening.

The caller hung up to her relief and disappointment. The call had been too long yet too short. Especially since she wanted—needed—answers.

Blood rushed wildly in her ears. It was the only thing she could hear in the quiet room. Feeling suffocated, she walked outside onto her small balcony, and inhaled the salty ocean air. Being near the ocean soothed her in a way nothing else did. Maybe because the ocean had saved her life in more ways than one. Her heartbeat slowed as she breathed in and out, taking deep, steadying breaths.

There was a slim chance the call was a prank, but the realistic part of her knew that was bullshit. And she couldn't lie to herself even if she wanted to.

She wrapped her arms around her chest and tried to block out the memories. Twelve years had passed and she could still feel his clumsy hands on her body. Could still smell the scotch on his breath. Dark spots briefly flashed in front of her vision and her throat clenched impossibly tight so she practiced her breathing techniques again until the weight lifted off her chest.

She turned back inside and went to the kitchen. As she prepared a pot of chamomile tea, an involuntary shiver raced down her spine. Past nightmares clawed at her memory.

She itched to call Mac and tell him about the call, but she would handle this on her own. As far back as she could remember she'd learned never to show fear. Fear was weakness. And the predators of the world preyed on the weak.

Never let them hear you scream and never let them see you cry. That was her motto.

Chapter 2

Two weeks later

Hope pulled her dark hair into a low twist as she walked along the rickety planks toward *Second Chance Marina*. April in Florida wasn't scorching, but summer was on its way and Key West heated up quicker than the rest of the state. She tripped on one of the boards still not fixed since the last hurricane and reeled in a curse.

Ever since her strange late night call a couple weeks ago, she'd been jumping at her own shadow. She absolutely hated that. Thankfully the more time that passed, the easier it was to distance herself from the call. Almost pretend it hadn't happened.

"Hey baby girl, the usual?" A familiar male voice called to her before she'd even made it to the thatch-roofed tiki bar that hung off the side of the main restaurant. Mac Jennings, the man who'd raised her since she was fifteen popped his head up from behind the main bar of the one-story structure. His sandy blond hair was just beginning to show signs of gray.

"Of course." She took a seat on one of the many empty high top stools and resisted the urge to lay her head down. Instead, she started making a pyramid out of the bar straws and matchbooks.

"Your burger should be ready in ten minutes."

"Don't forget extra pickles." She grinned and took a sip of the bottled water he placed in front of her.

"Long dive this morning?"

"Yeah, got some great pictures though." Her work as an underwater photographer was grueling, but she was already making a name for herself. Her portfolio had a long way to go, but her hard work was paying off and she wasn't even thirty.

"So what are you doing back so early?"

"I'm meeting some guy about doing contract work. My agent set it up. Some rich people down in Cuba want me to photograph their ancestral home or something. It's not underwater work, but this guy's wife apparently loves my prints."

"I'm so proud of you." He grinned and she fought the heat creeping up her neck and face. Mac had been an amazing surrogate father, teaching her how to survive, but he didn't give out compliments often. When he did, she was never sure how to react.

When she didn't respond he cleared his throat and glanced at his watch. "Food should be ready. But I think your 'rich guy' just arrived." Mac nodded to the other side of the bar as a man took a seat at one of the high top tables facing the open water.

It was only ten o'clock in the morning so the bar was empty. Chances were in her favor that this was the man she was waiting for. Even seated, he looked to be about six feet tall. His dark blue polo shirt stretched across broad shoulders. From her side view, his angular jaw looked like it had been chiseled from stone. The man had a perfect face for the camera.

She smiled when he looked up, finally noticing her. "Hi, I'm—"

"Maria? What are you doing here? I thought you were in California." His deep voice echoed loudly in the empty restaurant.

She turned around once to make sure he wasn't talking to someone else. When their gazes collided again, she lifted an eyebrow. "I'm Hope. Are you the man I'm supposed to meet? Lucas Romanov?"

When he simply stared, she decided he wasn't there to meet her after all. *Pity*, she thought. She'd love to snap some shots of him.

"Sorry to bother you," she murmured as she turned to head back to the bar.

"Wait." He reached out and clasped her upper arm. His fingers tightened for a brief instant before he pulled back.

She turned back to face him, her entire body tense, ready to strike out at him if necessary. Not that it mattered. Mac was within screaming distance and even though he was in his late fifties, the former Navy SEAL could hold his own against anyone.

The stranger stepped back immediately and lifted his hands in an apologetic gesture, but still stared at her with his dark, strangely haunting eyes.

"Sorry, I…you just remind me of someone. I am the man you're waiting for, but you can call me Luke. I didn't mean to scare you."

"Do you have any identification?" She crossed her arms over her chest, gauging his expression. She didn't care for weirdos who thought it was okay to touch people they'd just met. "As in a driver's license?"

He whipped out his wallet and shoved it at her, obviously trying to appease her. After looking at it, she handed it back to him. "Are you hungry or thirsty?"

He expelled a long breath. "I could go for a beer."

"Have a seat and I'll grab you one. Corona okay?" When he nodded, she returned to the bar. Normally she wasn't so bossy, but his reaction to meeting her had been weird. Not creepy, just a little strange. She had a very strong creep-meter and her alarm bells weren't going off.

"That him?" Mac asked as he placed a plate in front of her.

She nodded. "I didn't think he'd be early. And I'm going to have time to eat. Save it for me?"

When he shook his head and chuckled, she reached over the bar and grabbed two beers from the well. It was a little early, but what the heck, it was Saturday.

Seconds later she slid onto the seat across from Lucas Romanov and handed him his drink.

"You don't happen to know anyone named Maria, do you?" he asked.

She shook her head, even though the name triggered something vaguely familiar. She'd met a couple Maria's before, but she didn't actually know any. "Nope."

He expelled a long breath and laughed under his breath. "I swear you could pass for her twin sis..." He cocked his head to the side and his eyes darkened again.

Despite her best effort, she swallowed under his intense scrutiny. There was something about those charcoal eyes that made her think of sex and sin. A very bad thing considering the guy was married and her possible client. "You wanted to talk to me about a photography job for your wife?"

"My wife?" He chuckled. "I'm not married. I'm here as a favor to some friends."

"I don't understand. My agent told me you wanted me to—"

"I'm sorry, I thought this would have been explained to you. My friends, the Santiagos want to hire you. I work for them. Sonja, the wife, is a huge fan of your work. She insisted I come down here and personally take you to Cuba. She's very busy or she would have come herself."

"Which is it? You work for them or you're friends with them?" She took a sip of her beer and watched his eyes closely when he answered.

"Both. I'm head of their security, but our families have been friends since before I was born."

"Why do they need security?"

"They're very wealthy." He shrugged and even though his tone was casual, when he answered, she was under the distinct impression he was holding something back.

"Are they involved in drugs?"

His eyes widened, but a genuine smile played on his lips. He chuckled and his shoulders loosened a little. "No, coffee."

She gnawed on her bottom lip for a second. Her agent had okayed them and that was always good enough for her. "I was told this job is in Cuba?"

He nodded and a lock of his dark hair fell across his forehead. "That's right."

"When do they want me to start?"

He shifted in his seat and traced a finger down his beer bottle. "Honestly, they thought they'd have to wait to book you."

Sure, she worked for the Discovery Channel, something that always seemed to impress people, but she was a contract worker. That equaled a sporadic income. "Unfortunately I'm strictly a contract worker until I build up a bigger portfolio. I'm available to start in a couple days if they'd like." Actually she could start right then, but he hadn't asked. Her sales had doubled in the last month so she knew she was gaining popularity, but this kind of work could really boost her career.

"I'll call them today and set something up. How about we meet here tonight for dinner and discuss everything?"

She would have liked to discuss things right then, but he wasn't giving her much of a choice. "Seven works for me."

He drained the rest of his beer, then stood and left. As she watched him make his way out of the restaurant she chewed on her bottom lip. Her male friends, and the men she worked with, were unassuming and unthreatening in every way.

Lucas Romanov wasn't necessarily threatening, but he was still a stranger she knew nothing about. Without even trying, he exuded a raw, masculine power that was almost tangible. Not to mention something about that charcoal gaze made her feel unnerved. As if she were under a microscope.

And she liked to be in control.

* * * * *

Luke wiped sweaty palms on his jeans as he walked down Duval Street. Even though he'd had practically all day to clear his head, he opted to walk to the restaurant instead of drive. Meeting a woman who could be Maria Santiagos' twin disturbed him on too many levels. Maria's twin sister Anna had disappeared twenty-three years ago when she was just five years old.

And he'd never stopped blaming himself for it.

Loud island style tunes blared through the outside speakers as he walked up to the restaurant. The place was completely open and without central air, but a breeze from the Atlantic constantly blew through and huge fans had been set up in the four corners of the establishment.

Customers were three deep at the bar, but he spotted Hope Jennings immediately. He'd be blind not to. Even though she looked exactly like his childhood friend, he'd have noticed her anyway. Her startling pale, bluish gray eyes separated her from the crowd with their intensity. He'd never seen that exact color on anyone.

Except Maria and Sonja Santiago.

And of course Anna.

Though Sonja was Afghani, her skin was ivory pale. Her husband Jose was Cuban and naturally darker.

Maria had inherited traits from both her parents and while she had a golden glow year round, the woman he now stared at was a little darker and a lot leaner. Probably because she spent all her time in the sun. Other than those small differences, the two women had to be connected somehow.

His first instinct was to tell the Santiagos about Hope, but he couldn't get them excited with false dreams. Not after all they'd been through. He didn't know exactly what he was going to do, but he'd figure it out before they headed to Miami.

As if she knew she was being watched, Hope scanned the crowd, her eyes like heat seeking missiles. When she spotted him, she waved, dropped a quick kiss on the cheek of the older gentleman next to her, and fought through the throng of people toward him.

"You sure you want to have dinner here?" he shouted above the noise when she finally maneuvered her way through drunk, dancing people.

She just smiled and pointed behind him. "Follow me," she said.

Or at least that's what he thought she said.

They pushed through more people until they were outside and away from the mob.

"Where are we going?" he asked when she continued down one of the long wooden docks, away from the restaurant.

"There's an Irish pub a couple blocks from the marina. It's a lot quieter. Unless you want to stay here?" She paused and motioned behind them.

"No." He couldn't hear himself think, and a nice, quiet dinner with Hope didn't sound like a bad thing at all. It would give him a chance to pump her for information.

She didn't say much on their walk so he took the opportunity to steal glances at her profile. She'd worn a dark blue summer dress that tied around her neck and hugged her curves in all the right places. He also noticed she had a nasty scar on her right shoulder. The faded white cobwebbed marking was old, but was stark enough to make him wince. Whatever had happened to her, it had to have hurt. His first guess was a bullet wound, but that didn't seem likely considering she was a photographer. Even the thought of her being shot made something primal in him stir.

They stopped in front of what looked like an abandoned building. Hope grinned and opened one of the green doors.

"Trust me, the food here is great. Don't let the atmosphere fool you."

"Do we just seat ourselves?" He glanced around the dimly lit restaurant. There weren't any patrons and everything was green. The walls, the table cloths, even the hostess stand was the hideous color.

"Yes, they're not busy tonight so I don't think any hostesses are working."

He followed Hope and tried not to stare at her too much. He didn't want to come off like a pervert, but it still freaked him out how much she looked like Maria.

An Irish flag hung on the wall next to the booth they slid into. Though the dark cherry wood had a few nicks, it was definitely high quality.

A dark-haired man wearing a green Hawaiian T-shirt and cargo shorts appeared with two menus. "Can I get y'all drinks?"

"Corona," Hope said. He'd had her pegged as high maintenance, but that was probably because she looked so much like Maria.

"Same here."

The man winked at Hope, then looked him up and down with a cold stare before he turned and made his way across the room toward the bar. Seconds later he returned with identical beers.

"Thanks," Hope spoke to the bartender and took a sip of her beer. "Can you give us a couple minutes?"

Again the man nodded then left them alone.

"Come here often?"

She shrugged. "My dad owns this place and Frank knows what I like."

"Frank would be the bartender?" The man had disappeared behind the bar and was shouting something at a rugby match on one of the televisions.

"Well, he's the bartender and manager."

"So your dad owns this place, too?" He turned back to face her.

"Yes, in addition to the marina and this place, he owns one more restaurant."

"Is he the man you kissed earlier?" The question slipped out before he could censor himself.

Her dark eyebrows rose, but she answered. "Yep, that's my dad."

"You take after your mother?" The man he'd seen her with was about six feet tall, maybe in his fifties, and with his sandy blond hair and green eyes, they didn't look the least bit related. He knew it was a personal question and normally wouldn't have asked something like that, but he couldn't help it. Finding out everything there was to know about Hope had jumped to the most important thing in his life at the moment.

Her pale eyes narrowed. Instead of answering, she glanced at Frank, who was returning to take their orders.

"Y'all need a couple more minutes?" The man's thick southern drawl hung heavy in the air.

"I want my usual. Luke?"

"I'll take the special I saw on the board," he said and nodded at Frank, hoping for some kind of friendly response.

The man grunted at him and took the menus.

"Did I do something to piss him off?"

She chuckled. "He doesn't like strangers and he really doesn't like it when I date. You and I know this isn't a date, but he doesn't."

"Look, I think we might have gotten off on the wrong foot, so if I've done anything to make you feel uncomfortable, let me apologize now. I don't want my behavior to affect your decision to work for the Santiagos." He couldn't let her out of his sight until he knew if she had some sort of connection to them.

A small smile played on her lips. "Okay, you did kind of freak me out earlier, but I had my dad run your information and you check out."

He nearly choked on his beer. "You had me checked out?" Sure, he'd had one of his guys do a basic check of her too, but it surprised him she'd done the same.

She shrugged and her grin grew even wider. "Yes and I'd do it again. My agent said you were legit, but I wanted to be sure. Okay, let's get down to business. I want dates, information on where I'll be staying, the works. I don't like leaving anything to chance."

"Well, I spoke to Sonja today and she's willing to double what she was originally going to pay if you can leave tomorrow." He waited for a moment as she digested the information. He thought she would have probably gone for it anyway, but his employer was desperate to have Hope and only Hope.

Now he wondered if there was more to Sonja's insistence than she'd originally let on.

"Double? Why is this so important?" A discernable caution edged her voice.

Hope obviously didn't trust people and he couldn't blame her for being wary of him. "The Santiagos will be celebrating their thirtieth wedding anniversary and Sonja wants to surprise her husband."

"With pictures?"

He nodded. "Not just pictures. His home has been in their family for generations. Thanks to political contacts, even when Castro took over, they were able to keep their beach front property."

She let out a low whistle. "People would kill for real estate like that."

That was an understatement, but he chose not to comment directly. Instead, he gave her a lot more information than he needed to. He figured if he laid everything on the table, she'd realize he wasn't lying. "Even though they own the property in Cuba, they've lived in Jamaica for the past couple decades. They just bought a home in Miami. They're trying to settle in and she wants to decorate their new home completely in photographs from his family's ancestral home."

"Nice wife."

His voice softened when he spoke. "That she is." He started to say more when Frank returned with their food.

"When's their anniversary?" she asked as she picked up her fork.

"In a month."

"Jeez, no wonder she's willing to pay double." She chewed on her bottom lip for a moment, then asked, "Is that all?"

"No. When you're through, she also wants you to come to Miami to photograph her and their daughter."

Her shoulders lifted slightly. "I don't normally do portraits, but it won't be a problem."

He picked up his fork and stabbed a shrimp, hoping his relief wasn't obvious. Normally he didn't have a problem hiding his emotions, but her very presence threw him off kilter. "I thought you might have other work lined up, but this is great."

"Hey, as long as they pay for travel expenses, I wouldn't mind if they wanted me to go to China."

"Can you leave tomorrow?"

She nodded and took a bite of her coconut shrimp.

He cleared his throat and continued. "We can either fly into the Bahamas or Jamaica, and then head to Cuba, or we can sail there."

"Whatever works for you, but sailing is a lot quicker."

Well that was interesting. He'd expected more of a reaction. "You don't care that it's illegal to travel there?"

"Technically it's not illegal for me to be there. It's only illegal if I spend money there, and I don't plan to spend a dime. Our government has a lot more to worry about than American citizens visiting Cuba anyway." She took another bite of her shrimp and lifted her eyebrows at him.

"I take it you've been there before?"

"Sort of. I've gone diving off the coast of Cienfuegos a few times."

"How long have you been diving?"

"I guess about twelve years. I almost drowned when I was fifteen and when Mac…Mac taught me to swim and I literally took to it like a fish."

She probably didn't realize it, but her entire expression changed when she talked about her dad, and for a moment, she let him see a softer side. A side he very much wanted to get to know. Luke had to remind himself to breathe as he looked at her. "That's facing your fears head on." He took a bite of his shrimp pasta when he realized her age. She was twenty-seven. The same age as Maria.

Something solid settled in his gut. It couldn't be. The odds of finding Anna now were insane. Now, after years of searching and heartache.

"Luke?" Her voice startled him back to the present.

"What did you say?" How long had he been sitting there?

"Nothing, you're just looking at that plate of food as

14

if it holds the answers to life." Her pale eyes danced with laughter and his heart stuttered. Actually stuttered.

Which was all kinds of stupid.

He cleared his throat. "Sorry, I was just thinking we need to get an early start tomorrow if we want to make it by dark."

"So I take it we're sailing instead of flying?"

If it made the Santiagos happy, he'd get on a boat. In fact, it was the only reason in the world he'd do it. "Yes, but only because it's quicker."

"Tell me you don't get seasick."

He took a bite of his pasta and ignored her question. "I'd like to leave around seven tomorrow if that works for you."

"Sure. Where's the boat docked?"

"At your dad's marina."

Her eyes widened. "Are you the guy with the new Hatteras?"

"Well technically it's not mine, but yeah, that's what we'll be heading down in."

"I'm impressed." She pushed her empty plate away and leaned back in her seat.

Hell, he didn't even like boats, but hearing her say she was impressed did something to his ego. "What do you say we meet at the docks around seven tomorrow? It'll give us time to pack up your luggage and I'm sure you'll have a lot of photography gear."

She smiled and the sight made something inside him stir with primal awareness. "Perfect."

Chapter 3

Hope slipped off her sandals and curled her feet into the plush carpet of her condo. A couple hours to pack was more than enough time to get ready. Normally she only brought bathing suits and summer dresses when going on long dive trips, and she didn't plan to bring much more this time.

She automatically tensed as her house phone rang then wanted to curse. She didn't have caller ID, mainly because everyone she knew called her cell phone, and because her home phone was ancient. If she didn't need a land line for internet access, she'd get rid of it all together.

After staring at it for a few long seconds she snatched it up. "Hello?"

"How long are you going to be gone this time?"

She relaxed at hearing Mac's familiar voice, and threw another bathing suit into her bag. "A few weeks, maybe less. How'd you know I'd take the job, anyway?"

"It's a good opportunity, and you've got the travel bug…and it'll pay your rent for a few months."

She laughed under her breath. If it wasn't for Mac, she wouldn't have put down roots at all. Hell, if it wasn't for Mac she'd be at the bottom of the ocean. "I'll bring you back something, I promise."

"Just bring yourself back and promise to call when you get there. Don't make me send out a search party."

Seconds after they disconnected, the phone rang again. She picked up, a grin on her face. "Come on Mac, I promise to call. Lighten up."

Heavy breathing was the only response.

"Hello?" Her fingers tightened around the phone.

"You think you're safe? Your time is coming, bitch." His voice sounded slurred, as if he'd been drinking.

The phone line went dead before she got a chance to respond.

Fear snaked down her spine as she placed the phone back in its holder. Though she was tempted to call Mac, she didn't. But only because she was leaving in the morning. At least she'd be safe for a month. Once she got back, she'd try to figure out a way to deal with this. She started to throw another bathing suit into her bag, but decided to check her front door one more time. It was locked, so she slid the safety chain in place. It might not give her much extra protection, but it made her feel better.

* * * * *

Luke stood on the dock, waiting for Hope. His boat was docked right by the parking lot and she still hadn't shown up. It was only five after seven. Five minutes wasn't that late and it wasn't as if he knew her habits. For all he knew, she could be one of those women who showed up thirty minutes late for everything.

She was a complete and utter mystery. Now he was even more convinced she wasn't who she claimed to be. After dinner last night he'd called one of his contacts with the FBI to see what kind of information he could find on Hope. His friend had said he'd get back to him if he found any more information, but at first glance, it looked as if she'd appeared out of thin air around the age of fifteen.

As he waited, a dusty red jeep steered into the parking lot. Dust and gravel flew everywhere as the vehicle skidded to a halt in one of the empty spots. The windows were tinted, but the sporty jeep looked like something she'd drive. Seconds later Hope jumped out and waved to him. He walked down the dock and across the gravel lot to meet her.

"Everything okay?" He pulled two matching black bags from the back and she grabbed her purse, a skinny tripod bag, and two huge bags with camera equipment. He didn't see a laptop bag, though. He'd assumed she'd have one, especially if she used a digital camera, but maybe she was old school and used film.

"Yeah, why?"

He shrugged and took one of the big camera bags from her. What was he going to say? *Because you were five minutes late and I was worried.*

She caught on anyway. "You're on Key West time now, buddy. Trust me, I'm early."

One of the crew members helped her onto the back deck. He was just happy this crew was new and hadn't met Maria.

"Hi, I'm Hope." With a genuine smile, she extended a delicate hand to the man.

"Manuel." He held out a hand for her photography gear. "I'll put your things in your room."

She let go of her things reluctantly.

"They'll take good care of it, I promise." Luke placed her other bags onto the back deck because he knew one of the crew members would grab it in seconds. "Do you want to head up to the fly bridge or would you rather stay in the salon when we take off?"

She grinned and pointed up.

He climbed the ladder to the spacious deck ahead of

her. Under normal circumstances he would have let her go first, but she wore a loose summer dress that tied around her neck and he didn't think she'd appreciate him having a perfect shot of her—he swallowed hard and tried to scrub his wayward imagination. Not that it did any good. He still wondered what type of undergarments she wore, if any.

"So, do you think we'll have time to take a couple dive trips while we're there?" She took a seat on the cushioned bench and crossed her legs. Incredibly toned, sleek legs he had no problem imagining wrapped around his waist.

He leaned against one of the rails but shifted so that he wasn't directly facing her. He needed to get himself under control. His physical reaction to her disturbed him, made him feel less in control. "I don't see why not. There's certainly enough gear on this boat."

"Great." She smiled and leaned back in her seat.

He turned and faced the open water. The boat rumbled beneath them and he tried to focus on the crystal clear water in front of him.

"It's beautiful isn't it?" Hope asked as she leaned against the rail next to him.

Luke was slipping. He hadn't even felt her move up behind him. When her arm pressed against his, he told himself to move away but couldn't force himself to do it.

"Yes." He shifted his position and inadvertently inhaled her sweet scent. She smelled like the beach. Tropical, fresh, and something else indefinable.

Something that was all Hope.

* * * * *

Patrick Taylor opened his eyes to a loud banging. Struggling to shove the tangled sheets off his body, he managed to roll over. He thought he'd brought someone home last night but his bed was empty. After a three day bender, his whole body ached. The banging continued, and when his father's angry voice carried through the front door of the condo to his back bedroom, he stumbled out of bed. His stomach roiled, but he ignored it. His father, the 'great' Richard Taylor, did not like to wait.

"Prick," he muttered under his breath.

Not bothering to put on clothes, he rushed down the long hallway to the tiled entrance and opened the door wearing only boxers. "What the hell is it this time?" For once, he was glad he didn't have a woman over. No one to see his father humiliate him.

His father ignored his question and brushed past him. Having no choice, Patrick followed him to the kitchen.

"Do I have to do everything myself?" his father demanded.

Patrick leaned against one of the granite counters and rubbed a hand over his face. There was a coat of fur across his teeth. A toothbrush would help. Then coffee and a fucking bottle of aspirin to get rid of this headache. "What are you talking about this time?"

His father pulled out a picture and threw it on the counter next to him. "I'm talking about this."

He glanced at it and fought the urge to punch something. It was *her*. The bitch who had scarred his face. "I told you I'd take care of it." He'd already put in a few late night calls to rattle her. He wanted that bitch to *know* he was coming, and that there was nothing she could do about it. Last night he'd intended to taunt her longer but he'd been too drunk to carry on a conversation.

"You've had three days and my sources tell me you've been partying instead." His father slammed his fist down on the counter. "I've got enough crap to deal with lately and don't want to involve my men, but if you can't handle this on your own, then—"

"I can handle it!"

"Good. There's a car waiting for you downstairs. You have twenty minutes."

The last thing he wanted to do was bother with this mess now, but what choice did he have? He'd planned to make her sweat for a couple weeks before he headed down to The Keys. Twelve years had passed, a couple more days wouldn't hurt.

His father started to leave, but paused in the doorway of the kitchen. "Don't fuck this up. If you do…"

He didn't finish, but Patrick knew what he meant. His father was tired of his 'fuck-ups' and had told him too many times to count. Patrick doubted he'd think twice about getting rid of him, too. In his bedroom, he haphazardly shoved clothes in a duffel bag. He didn't plan to be gone long. He'd clean up his mess, then come back home and pick up right where he'd left off.

When he went to retrieve his toiletry bag from the bathroom he glanced in the mirror and unwanted anger bubbled up inside him. Thanks to the best surgeons on the East Coast, a faded white line on his cheek bone was the only visible marking from his…injury. It still pissed him off, but most days he could forget about it entirely.

He still couldn't believe he'd found her. On a random website for photography of all things. Maybe the fates were finally smiling down on him.

For once.

Now that bitch was going to pay. Though he hated to admit it, his father was probably right. He needed to take care of her now. And after he found her, he could have some fun with her before killing her once and for all.

* * * * *

"Okay, I've got to ask. How is it that your employers

21

still have a house in Cuba?" Five hours later, Hope eyed the palatial home on the private beach where they'd docked. The house was impressive, but the view more so. They had prime beach front property with no visible neighbors for miles. She'd thought it odd when Luke told her they had property in Cuba, but now that she viewed it, she was even more suspicious.

"Money." Luke's answer was short and to the point as he headed down the dock, but nowhere near the answer she was looking for.

At first she hadn't minded coming to Cuba considering she'd done it before, but this house screamed money. And not the kind of money you made selling coffee. "I thought you said they were involved in coffee." Instead of following, she stayed put.

With his bag and one of her bags slung over his shoulder he turned, frustration written in every line of his face. "They have plantations in Jamaica, Brazil, and Costa Rica. Now can we please get settled in? I'd like to show you around before tomorrow."

Purse in hand, she fell in step with him. Now it actually made sense that the family needed security. They weren't just wealthy, they were probably listed in Forbes as some of the richest people on the planet. Which left more than a couple of questions.

Why on earth would they have hired her when they could literally have anyone? And why hadn't her agent told her any of this?

She ignored the sudden flutter in her stomach and followed Luke along the sturdy dock toward the large, Spanish-style house. An Olympic-size swimming pool sat in the middle of a well-maintained garden. As they neared the stone veranda attached to the back of the house, she noticed a tray of refreshments and assorted fruit laid out on a glass and metal table.

"Is someone expecting us?"

He nodded. "Yes, I called ahead while you were taking pictures."

Luke opened one of the French doors into what she guessed to be a formal sitting room and followed her inside. "Wait here for a minute?" he asked.

As he disappeared down a marble hallway, Hope absently nodded and took in her surroundings. This room would be perfect to start photographing.

She took a careful seat on a high-backed armchair. Wall-to-wall windows filled the room with light. A wood plank ceiling and ornate, brass light fixtures gave the room a vintage feel even though the furniture was modern and probably new. A sofa and two armchairs were positioned around a cherry wood coffee table perfectly centered in the room. Against one of the walls, a hutch displayed different pieces of china. As she glanced around the room, she couldn't shake the feeling of familiarity. The thought itself was crazy, but a strange awareness settled in her gut. Bone deep and almost chilling with its intensity.

"Hope?" Luke's deep voice nearly made her jump.

"Yes?" She immediately stood, thankful for the interruption.

"Your room is ready, but if you'd rather tour the grounds we can start now."

"I'm ready, but I'd really like to speak to Sonja Santiago about what exactly she wants." In truth, she wanted to get out of the room and away from the iciness that was slowly snaking its way down her spine.

"What do you mean?"

"Well, I know what you've told me, but doesn't she want to talk to me, first? It just seems odd that she's trusting me to do this big job without going over any details." Everything had happened so fast, Hope hadn't thought much about it until they were half way to Cuba.

He shrugged. "That's why she sent me. She's seen

your portfolio and she's impressed."

"If you don't think it's necessary, then I guess it's okay." It wasn't as if she had any reason to complain. They'd already deposited half her fee into her checking account, and her agent had told her they were on the up and up. Still, she couldn't shake the feeling that something was off.

"Here." He held out one of her photography bags. "You can leave your purse here."

He held the French door open for her again, and the old-fashioned gesture warmed her heart. She didn't trust easily, and even though Luke had an intimidating look about him, her intuition told her he'd never hurt her. On the trip over she'd had a brief moment of panic at being stuck with a strange male in a strange house in a strange country, but it quickly vanished. She didn't know why, but when he looked at her, she experienced a vague sense of security.

"Have you spent a lot of time here?" she asked as they walked through the garden, circling the house. Iron gates surrounded the majority of the property, but it was obviously for decoration, as it didn't completely enclose the back.

"I spent a lot of my childhood here. Until I was thirteen. My parents and I would often vacation here a couple weeks out of the year." His words were clipped and that surprised her. It was a simple question. Since the afternoon sun beat down on them, he'd put on sunglasses. She didn't like it that she couldn't see his eyes.

"Why'd you stop coming here?" She paused mid-stride and snapped a few pictures of the back of the house, capturing the sweeping lawn.

"Life got in the way. There's one more place I want to show you, then I'll let you do your job."

They walked past oversized hedges and into a hidden

rose garden. A gasp escaped before Hope could contain herself. She almost dropped her camera as she reached for Luke's arm.

He stiffened beside her and said something but she couldn't make out the jumble of his words.

The lush garden with its vibrant colors and sweeping pathways was a photographer's dream, but that wasn't what had shocked her. A vision had flashed in her mind so vivid she clutched his arm to keep her knees from buckling. *Two little girls in matching dresses threw a beach ball back and forth. People were laughing and drinking and other children were running around, but the two little girls weren't paying any attention to anyone else. They were too caught up in their game.*

She didn't have memories of her childhood. Even her time in the foster system was scratchy until she turned about eight or nine. That first year was a blur of caseworkers and foster parents. Vague snatches occasionally popped into her mind. She often dreamed about a woman singing her to sleep, but the memories were fuzzy. Possibly not even real. Still, she could almost swear one of the little girls she'd just seen had been herself. Which was impossible, if not insane.

"Are you okay?" He took his sunglasses off and turned so that he held her by the shoulders. Tingles shot down her arm. She never allowed virtual strangers to touch her, but at the moment, she needed it.

For a moment she struggled to breathe, but his firm grip steadied her. "I'm fine." Heat rushed to her cheeks, but there wasn't anything she could do about it. This was the most money she'd made on one job and she didn't want to screw it up.

"Are you sure you're okay? Do you want me to get you some water?" His deep voice somehow grounded her.

"No, I think I just got a little overheated, that's all."

She let out a self-deprecating laugh, hoping he believed her. On her dive trips, she spent days out in the sun. It was something she was used to. Maybe he wouldn't realize that.

His charcoal eyes studied her, as if he could read her thoughts until finally he released her. Her body mourned the loss of those strong, steadying hands on her bare skin. It was almost like he'd branded her with that simple touch. Feeling her face heat, she dipped her gaze to avoid his, and made the mistake of noticing his lips. An unexpected jolt of awareness shot through her, straight to all her nerve endings. She'd been aware that he was good looking—especially since she was a photographer—but knowing something and having her body realize it were two different things. She was just as appreciative of a fine male specimen as the next woman, but actually being aware of one man was rare. Very rare. Right now it was so easy to imagine what it would feel like to have those full lips pressed to hers. Her fingers balled into fists and she had to stop herself from reaching out and touching him. She cleared her throat and started to say something but Luke smiled tightly then stepped back.

"I'll be in the house if you need me."

Before she could think to ask where her room was, he'd disappeared through the hedges.

* * * * *

Luke hurried back to the Santiagos' villa. Away from the woman with the big eyes that called to all his protective instincts. Hope had looked terrified, not overheated. Something had happened out there and for whatever reason, she'd lied to him. He'd probably scared the hell out of her, grabbing hold of her like a monk who hadn't touched a woman in a decade, but something about her called out to his most primitive side. He wanted to stroke and kiss every inch of her body.

As he walked onto the veranda, his cell phone buzzed. "Hi Sonja."

"Hello Lucas." Even if his caller ID hadn't told him who was calling, her soft Afghani accent was unmistakable. Though she'd lived between the Caribbean and the United States for years, she'd never lost that distinctive speech pattern.

"Is everything okay?" he asked immediately. Sonja rarely checked up on him. Normally when she asked him to do something, she let him do his job. Family friend or not, he wasn't going to be micromanaged.

"Of course, I'm just checking in to make sure you arrived safely."

"We got here about an hour ago and she's already started working."

"Wonderful…what is she like?"

"She seems to know what she's doing."

"Oh." Her voice had a touch of disappointment.

"She's who you wanted, right? You haven't changed your mind?"

"No! I mean, no, of course not. I just wanted to know if…uh…"

Realization slammed into him. "Sonja? Is there something you're not telling me?"

"Well…I thought maybe she might remind you of someone."

"Shit." He never cursed around Sonja because he knew she despised it.

"She looks just like Maria, doesn't she?" Sonja continued, almost breathless.

She did, but he wasn't ready to confirm it yet. "Is that why you sent me? You *knew* about this?" A head's up would have been nice.

"I couldn't come, myself. I was looking for

photographers and when I saw her picture on her website I almost had a heart attack. I didn't trust myself to see her in person. I thought maybe you'd be objective enough—" Her voice broke off into a half-sob and Luke's heart twisted. "I can't get my hopes up again after all these years. My heart can't take it. That's why I sent you, don't you understand?" The agony in her voice clawed at his insides.

He scrubbed a hand over his face. "Unfortunately, I do."

A few moments passed, but he figured she needed to compose herself. Eventually she continued. "Does she look like her? Now that you've seen her in person?"

He couldn't lie to her. Not that it would matter if he did. He'd be bringing Hope to Miami in a week or two, anyway. "There are differences…but yes, she does have some similarities to Maria." There were a lot more than *similarities* between the two, but he couldn't bring himself to voice it aloud just yet. He needed to see Hope next to Maria.

Sonja expelled a long sigh. He wasn't sure if it was out of relief or panic. Maybe it was a bit of both. "Do you think it's…it's my Anna?"

"I honestly don't know." If he gave her false hope after all these years and he was wrong, he couldn't live with himself. "Have you told anyone else about her?"

"No. I didn't want to upset Jose or Maria if it wasn't necessary. I don't think poor Jose's heart would be able to take it. And Maria has dealt with enough over the years."

For a woman who'd lost her daughter, she'd never given up hope that Anna was alive. She'd had a few breakdowns over the years, and at one point Luke had been sure Sonja and Jose would divorce, but she'd tried her best to raise Maria with a sense of normalcy.

Unlike her, Luke had buried Anna's ghost a long

time ago. Or at least he thought he had until he'd come face to face with Hope. "What are you going to do when I bring her to Miami?"

"I have no idea." She sighed, the sound heavy and tired.

That's what he was afraid of. "I'm going to see what information I can dig up, but I'll call you soon."

As soon as they disconnected, he dialed another number. He wanted to check in with his FBI contact. Hopefully he'd have news about Hope's background. His friend, Max Gray, picked up on the third ring. "Gray here."

"Hey, Max, I was just calling to check—"

"Look, I'm swamped right now. I'll call you back later."

Luke paused for a second. He and Max went back about a decade. Before he had a chance to respond, Max hung up.

What the hell was that? Luke stared at his phone for a second before retreating inside.

In his room, he changed into jogging clothes. Too many questions raced through his head. Maybe if he worked out he'd be able to work out some of his tension. Though, somehow he doubted it.

As he left his room, the buzz of his phone stopped him. He didn't know the number, but recognized the area code. "This is Luke."

"It's Max." His voice was low, almost a whisper.

"Man, what the hell is going on?"

"Listen, I don't have long, I'm calling from a payphone if you can believe that. Whatever you've gotten yourself into, keep me out of it." A horn blasted in the background.

"What?"

"That girl you wanted me to check out, Hope Jennings, well forget about it." Though Max's voice was low, Luke didn't miss the anxiety.

"Why?"

"About an hour after I started digging, the Deputy Director himself strolled into my cubicle."

"What?" An icy fist clasped around his heart.

"The only thing I managed to find out is that Mac Jennings was a SEAL in 'Nam and he's got friends in high places. Really high. And not just with the bureau. If you've got contacts with the CIA, be careful who you ask. I've got to go." His friend disconnected again.

Luke frowned at his silent cell phone. One thing he was sure of, one way or another, he was going to find out who the hell Mac and Hope Jennings were. He'd expected roadblocks, but this wasn't even in the realm of what he thought he'd be up against.

Which only intrigued him more.

Maybe he'd go straight to the source and just ask Hope. He snorted as the thought instantly dissipated. If he did that, she was likely to split. Hell, there was no likely about it. She would. Then he'd never get his answers. And the Santiagos would never know the truth. More than anything their family deserved closure about their missing daughter. And if it turned out Hope was her... Luke wouldn't let himself go there. Not yet.

Chapter 4

Hope spent the next couple of hours walking the main grounds and the private beach, snapping shots from every angle possible. She doubted she'd need a full two weeks to photograph everything, but she wanted a solid week so she could shoot at different times during the day.

As she walked across the backyard she noticed Luke standing on a small balcony. *Without a shirt.* He was on his cell phone and so engrossed in his conversation he wasn't aware of her presence. She studied his lean form and flat, muscular profile. He was in good shape, but she doubted he frequented gyms. He didn't seem the type. No, he probably got his exercise outside…or maybe in the bedroom.

Her stomach clenched as the random thought of tangled sheets and their sweaty bodies intertwined made its way to the forefront of her brain. On impulse she took a few covert shots of him. With his structured face and defined body, the man was extremely photogenic.

That wasn't why she'd taken the pictures though, and she knew it.

Sighing, she put the lens cap back on her trusty Nikon and went inside. She heard singing from somewhere as she worked her way through the house, trying to find where her room was. As she walked down a long tiled hallway, she couldn't help but notice how bare everything was. Sure, the house was nicely decorated, but there were no pictures or mementos anywhere.

Her sandals clicked along the floor until she found the source of the singing. A petite, dark-skinned woman was shaking her hips and moving around the kitchen as she cooked and sang. Hope paused in the archway for a moment, not wanting to disturb her. The woman in the ankle length dress had to be in her late sixties, but she danced around the kitchen with graceful ease.

Hope stepped onto the mosaic tile and cleared her throat, meaning to ask for directions to her room. When the woman turned from the stove, Hope smiled and walked toward her. "Hi, I'm Hope. I'm staying here with Luke."

The woman's face faded to an ashen gray. She then crossed herself, and grabbed one of Hope's hands. She started mumbling something indiscernible and her grip tightened.

Hope took a step back and tried to wrench free. What was it with strangers who thought it was okay to just touch her?

"Zara."

Luke's deep voice caused Hope to jump. She hadn't even heard him enter the room. The woman dropped her hand as he said something in a language Hope couldn't understand. Hope quickly shifted away to stand by Luke.

"I think she's confused," she murmured just low enough for him to hear.

He stepped in front of her, half blocking her from the other woman.

"Dinner will be ready in a couple hours. Do you want to freshen up?" Luke asked in equally quiet tones.

She nodded and glanced back and forth between the

other woman and Luke. "Is she okay?"

He nodded, but she didn't miss the strain in his dark eyes. "She's fine."

Out of natural curiosity Hope wanted to question further, but realized it wasn't her place. She was hired to do a job, nothing more. "Where's my room?"

"Make a left out of here. At the end of the hallway you'll see a winding staircase. Your room is the second door on the left."

"Where's your room?"

His eyebrows lifted slightly, but he answered neutrally. "Third door on the left. Next to yours."

She found it just as he'd said. Her room was also tiled, like the rest of the house, in a basic taupe color, but maroon and gold throw rugs brightened the floor. Her bags were on the bench at the foot of the queen-size poster bed so she grabbed what she needed and headed for the bathroom.

Over dinner she planned to find out anything she could about Luke Romanov. It wasn't any one thing in particular, but she knew he was keeping something from her.

And she didn't like it one bit. She knew it was the control freak inside her and that she should just do her job, get paid and go home, but that so wasn't going to happen.

* * * * *

Luke stared out the high windows of the dining room as he waited for Hope. He'd wanted to have a more intimate atmosphere for dinner, but Zara had insisted they eat in the formal dining area. He'd conceded because she'd threatened him with an infertility curse. Not that he actually believed in that stuff, but still, he wasn't taking any chances. Thank God the woman barely spoke English. When he'd walked in to the kitchen earlier and heard her mumbling in Creole to Hope that she was a miracle, his heart had sped up.

Then reality sank in and he'd realized Hope couldn't understand her.

"Is this where we're eating?" Hope's soft voice jarred him out of his thoughts.

He turned around and sucked in a breath. The light streaming in from the windows flickered off the chandelier, illuminating her delicate features. She wore a simple green sleeveless dress that fell right at her ankles. It wasn't tight, but when she moved, the soft material swayed against her body, revealing the lean lines of her body. It took him a moment for it to register that she'd asked him something. "I'm sorry what?"

She smoothed down her dress self-consciously. "I asked if I should sit."

"Yes, sorry. Normally it's not so formal, but you're a guest so Zara wanted to do something big." He led her to the end of the cherry wood rectangular table and sat directly across from her.

Luke shot Zara a warning look as she entered carrying two covered dishes. He'd had a talk with her about Hope. He didn't want her gushing all over her again. Not until he figured out a few things.

Hope moved to help Zara, but he cleared his throat, and she stopped. "Don't, she'll be offended."

She remained immobile, but he could tell she felt uncomfortable. After two more trips, the table was full of rice, beans, empanadas, and everything else Anna had liked as a child. *Subtle.* Zara threw him a haughty glare before returning to the kitchen. He couldn't blame her for being pissed at him, but he couldn't have her spooking Hope.

"Those are *maduros*." He pointed to one of the smaller dishes.

She smiled and scooped some on her plate. "I know. They're my favorite."

"You speak Spanish?" He tried to keep his tone casual.

"A little. I'm not fluent, but enough to get by." She took a bite and he nearly forgot to breathe at the pure pleasure that played across her features. She let out a sigh and when her tongue flicked out over her bottom lip, his entire body tensed in anticipation. He could watch her eat all day.

"What about you?" she asked after she swallowed.

He nodded, but didn't further elaborate.

"What else do you speak?" she prodded.

"Why do you assume I speak more languages?"

She lifted her eyebrows and took another bite.

"Okay, I also speak Russian and a little Creole."

"And that's what Zara was speaking earlier?" She motioned toward the kitchen entrance with her hand.

He nodded and started to ask another question but she beat him to it. "So how is it that you're friends with the Santiagos?"

"My parents introduced Sonja to Jose."

She nodded and asked another question. "How is it that Zara works here full time when they rarely come here?"

"She doesn't. She lives in Jamaica on their main estate. She just came here to get the house ready, but she'll be leaving in the morning."

Hope squirmed in her seat and Luke could practically see the gears turning in her head. He guessed she was trying to think of more questions to ask in an effort to avoid answering his.

If this had been any other woman he would have used his charm to get answers from her. Unfortunately he couldn't do that. Not if there was a chance she was Anna.

"Why did you go into security?" Her question was casual, but an underlying current of something he couldn't define passed between them. As if she was testing him.

"Because the world needs it. I'll never be out of a job."

"But you don't just do security do you?"

"What?"

"Sorry, I'm not trying to be nosy. I told you I had Mac run your information and he mentioned that you also worked with an organization in Miami that searches for missing children. I was just curious why. It's…it's an odd thing to do unless you've lost someone and Mac said you hadn't." Those exotic bluish-gray eyes stared at him in open curiosity.

Well, it certainly wasn't for the money. All his work was pro bono. He donated about a month of his time every year and whatever resources he could the rest of the year. "Because I can." This was supposed to be about her. How had she managed to turn the tables on him?

Despite the burning need to fire personal questions at her, he decided to keep things neutral. For the moment anyway. "How did you end up working as a photographer?"

The movement was faint, but she leaned back, slightly relaxing in her seat. "After two years of college I realized it wasn't for me so I signed up for cosmetology school. That *definitely* wasn't my thing."

"Cosmetology school?" Somehow he couldn't see her styling hair and doing nails.

A small smile tugged at her lips. "Yeah. The first time I had an 'accident', I got a warning, but the second time I screwed up, they kicked me out."

"What exactly did you do?"

Laughter danced in her eyes as she answered. "The first time I burned off a girl's hair."

"What?"

"Not all of it. In my defense she didn't tell me that she'd had it colored a couple days before coming in to see me. She wanted the color changed, but didn't realize she had to wait."

"How did you get kicked out?"

She cleared her throat and her cheeks turned a bright shade of pink. "I started a little fire."

"Shit."

"Exactly. And this time, it was definitely my fault. I left a hot hair straightener on a towel. It was just supposed to be for a second, but I got a phone call and forgot about it. I don't think I would have lasted much longer anyway."

He knew he should be drilling her for answers about her father, but he found himself smiling as she opened up to him. "That's impressive."

She chuckled and speared a piece of chicken with her fork. "That's exactly what Mac said." Before taking a bite she asked, "What about you? Ever burn a building down?"

"Nothing like what you did, but I did cause a small explosion in my high school chemistry class. I was grounded for a month after that one. Almost missed prom because of that one." It wasn't in his nature to open up to strangers, but he knew the only way to gain her trust was to do just that. And he found he liked her knowing more about him too.

Hope chuckled under her breath and shook her head. "At least you made it to prom."

"You didn't go to yours?" It was hard to imagine her not having *multiple* offers.

"No. I broke my leg two days before."

"How?"

"I was at a friend's house and someone got the bright idea that we could jump off the roof into the pool. After this guy Jimmy Carver made it, I tried it." She shuddered as she scooped rice onto her fork. "My dad was really pissed over that. But since I missed prom and I couldn't go diving for a couple months, he figured that was punishment enough."

"So how'd you end up in photography?"

She shrugged. "I sort of fell into it. Diving and swimming are like breathing to me. After I got kicked out of cosmetology school, I signed up for a couple photography classes and something clicked."

"You're obviously doing something right. I've seen your portfolio and it's impressive."

Her cheeks reddened at his words, but she didn't respond.

Since they'd been talking about safe subjects she'd been relaxed. Open with him even. Luke decided to risk asking a more personal question. "Why do you call your dad Mac?"

For a split second some indiscernible emotion flashed in her eyes, but she recovered quickly with a casual shrug. "Everyone calls him that."

Okay, not exactly a straight answer. He'd try another angle. "For someone who just owns a couple restaurants, he certainly seems to have a lot of contacts."

"What do you mean?" She took another bit of food.

"He'd have to know certain people to run my information and get actual answers. How's that possible?"

She cleared her throat. "He was in the Navy." The words were said so absolutely, as if that should explain everything.

Which, in a way it did. If her father had been a lifer, then he'd have had to make some serious contacts. So, he didn't push the issue. He'd wait until the time was right.

With her fork, she shoved her food around her half

empty plate. Great, now he'd made her lose her appetite. The opposite of what he wanted to do. "Do you feel like taking a walk on the beach after dinner?"

Their gazes collided and for a moment, he thought she'd say yes.

"I'm pretty beat, but maybe tomorrow. I want to get up early anyway and get some morning photos." She stood uncertainly. "Should I leave this stuff or…"

"It's fine." He put his fork down as she left and rubbed a hand over his face. This wasn't going at all as he'd   planned.

* * * * *

Luke opened his eyes, instantly alert. A scream ripped through the air and twenty-three years worth of built up guilt shredded through him.

It was Hope.

He grabbed his SIG from the nightstand and rushed to her bedroom. With caution, he eased open her door, but paused in the doorway.

Her balcony door was open, and the moonlight streamed through, illuminating her lean form. Hope was asleep in bed, but mumbling and thrashing around. The sheet tangled around her legs. He laid his gun on the bureau next to the door. It wouldn't serve to freak her out even more. With measured movements, he sat on the bed and gently touched her shoulder.

"Hope, wake up."

She opened her eyes, then opened her mouth as if to let out another scream, but stopped suddenly. Her entire body was tense as she glanced around in confusion. "What…is everything okay? Why are you here?"

"You screamed." He didn't know what else to say.

She sat up and shoved the sheet off her. A sheen of sweat covered her face, and her breathing was erratic, but she didn't push him away. If anything, she seemed relieved to have him present. Though he doubted she'd admit it.

"Sorry about that," she mumbled. She pulled back as if suddenly embarrassed, and retreated to the bathroom. He watched as she walked away from him. She wore skimpy blue shorts that barely covered her butt and a matching skin-tight tank top. It was hard not to imagine what it would be like to peel her barely-there clothes away and see what he'd been fantasizing about before she'd woken him up.

He heard the sound of running water, then moments later she was back. "I didn't mean to wake you."

He stood, figuring she wanted some privacy. "It's no problem. Are you okay? That was some scream."

It was hard to tell in the dark, but it almost looked like she blushed. "Yeah, sorry again. I haven't had a...it's been a long time since I've had a nightmare that bad."

"Want to talk about it?" He already knew the answer before he asked, but he had to try. The reason he wanted to know had nothing to do with helping the Santiagos. His protective instincts had kicked into high gear and he simply wanted to comfort her.

She shook her head and wouldn't meet his gaze as she climbed back into bed. He just stood there, knowing he should leave, but he couldn't bring himself to abandon her.

As if she'd read his mind, she said, "I'm fine, I promise. You can go back to sleep with no worries. Trust me, I've never had more than one in a night."

He stood off to the side of the bed and when she finally looked at him, his gut clenched. She stared at him with those big pale eyes, looking at him as if she knew real monsters existed. Something deep inside him twisted. "If you don't mind, I'll just sit here for a few minutes." He gestured to the rocking chair in the corner of the room.

"That's not necessary."

She was embarrassed, but he didn't care. He couldn't leave her now. Not after what he'd seen.

"It's not for you. It's for me, I'll feel better."

Her eyes narrowed in disbelief, but she finally lay back, then curled into the fetal position. He thought he heard her mumble something under her breath, but he couldn't be sure.

A couple minutes later, her voice cut through the quiet night air. "Are you awake?"

"Yeah."

She sighed and rolled onto her back. It was dark, but he could tell she was staring at the ceiling. "I hate when this happens."

"Sure you don't want to talk about it?"

"Yes, I'm sure. I'm just frustrated that my body is tired, but my head won't let me sleep." She rolled over on her side so she faced him.

Even though he could barely see her face, he could feel her eyes on him. "Want to talk about something else then?"

"Like what?"

"I don't know." He racked his brain for a safe topic. "Favorite movies?"

"I bet you're into action movies," she murmured as she shifted against the pillows.

He smiled into the darkness. "Close. Thrillers. And I bet you don't even like movies all that much?"

A soft laugh escaped. "Yeah, you're more likely to catch me watching a nature documentary than anything else."

Her small admission wasn't surprising. When she didn't continue, he laid his head back against the chair. A few minutes later though, she spoke again. "You really don't have to stay, Luke. I promise I'll be okay."

He paused for a long beat, then did something he'd never done before. "Before I was in security, I was in the Marines. The majority of my time in the Corps I spent in Africa. Djibouti to be exact." Technically his team had been stationed in Djibouti, but they'd spent weeks and months on recon missions scattered across the continent. He couldn't tell her that though.

"Yikes," she murmured.

Not exactly how he'd put it, but he silently agreed. The place was a shithole. "My first year back in civilian life, I couldn't sleep for shit. I was lucky if I got a solid three hours during the night."

"How'd you get over it?"

"Time."

"Did you... have nightmares too?"

"Sometimes." More often than he'd admit. He'd never woken up screaming, but he had awakened to find himself drenched in sweat too many times to count. Something he'd never told another soul. Not even his parents. He'd been barely twenty two when he'd returned home and everyone had expected him to be exactly the same. So, he'd kept that shit to himself.

"Do you want to talk about it?"

He chuckled under his breath. "Not really."

"Sorry, I wasn't being a smartass. I was—"

"I know you weren't." She might be a damn mystery, but one thing he was sure about. The woman was sincere.

"For what it's worth, I'm sorry for whatever you went through." Her voice was quiet.

The words shouldn't be significant, but they were because she meant it. She might not have a clue what he'd gone through, but it was obvious she was a survivor. Something he should have recognized sooner.

She shifted back into the fetal position and this time

she didn't talk or move again.

After half an hour, the steady sound of her breathing was the only sound in the room, but he didn't leave. Watching her sleep, an odd protectiveness filled him.

Something had changed—a subtle shift inside him and in his relationship with Hope—and he wasn't sure why. Even though he couldn't put his finger on it, he felt the change bone deep and it scared the shit out of him.

* * * * *

Hope opened her eyes to the new surroundings and rolled onto her back. She was alive. She wasn't bleeding and floating to a watery grave. Something she often had to remind herself. She hadn't had a nightmare like the one last night in months. And she was embarrassed it had happened here of all places.

A slight movement out of the corner of her eye caught her attention. Luke was still in her room. Sitting on the old wooden rocking chair he looked cramped and uncomfortable. One leg was thrown over the armrest and he cuddled a red decorative throw pillow with gold fringe. His face was all angles and harsh lines, but asleep he lost some of those qualities. Maybe it had something to do with the ridiculous pillow he clutched, but somehow he was less threatening.

She couldn't believe he'd stayed with her. Her throat tightened at the thought, but she shoved those emotions away. He wasn't being protective. He'd just fallen asleep. As quietly as possible, she sat up and eased out of bed. The minute her feet touched the floor, his eyes opened.

She froze, as if she was an intruder. "Hi?" It came out as a question.

He yawned and raked a hand through his hair before standing and stretching. "Morning. Can't believe I managed to sleep in that chair." He shook his head and rubbed a hand over his face, still half asleep.

"Me either." She chuckled, and some of her self-consciousness ebbed away, but she felt her face heat up as she drank in the sight of him. When she'd seen him on the balcony without a shirt, the distance had been a nice barrier. Up close and personal, she had to remind herself to breathe. All those muscles just begged to be touched. Her fingers actually itched to stroke over his chest and the incredible tight planes of his stomach. A very thin line of dark hair tracked down his muscular abdomen to the top of his boxers. To her horror, her face flamed as she wondered what he would look like underneath that flimsy barrier. Yeah, she needed to rein her thoughts in if she wanted to keep a professional atmosphere.

She quickly averted her gaze to his face, only to realize he was assessing her, too. His eyes darkened when they rested on her lower body.

Instinctively she covered her upper thigh with her hand. His intense scrutiny reminded her of her hideous scar. She'd had it for so long now she was almost able to forget it existed. Luke's dark eyes met hers, but she couldn't read him. She wondered what he was thinking, then inwardly cursed. She shouldn't care. She'd never cared before. It was a part of her. If someone was disgusted by it, then screw them.

Luke broke the silence, his voice raw. "I know you probably want to get started, but if you need me, I'll be around the house." He started to leave, but she stopped him.

"Thank you for…" she waved her hand in the air, unable to finish.

Instead of making her feel stupid, he surprised her. His features softened and his lips curved into a small smile. "Anytime."

* * * * *

Patrick threw back another scotch. He could have handled this on his own. He signaled to one of the crew members on his father's yacht that he wanted another drink.

When the man hesitated, he slammed his fist down on the cushiony chair. "Now!"

After his refill he leaned back and stretched out on the top deck. It didn't matter if he was drunk, anyway. His father had insisted on letting his men take care of things so Patrick wouldn't screw anything up. Despite the fact that he'd told Patrick to handle this on his own, at the last minute, he'd sent some of his thugs to tag along. His father just assumed he'd screw up. Patrick wondered why his father even kept him around.

"Maybe you should lay off." John, his father's right-hand man sat next to him and placed a hand on his shoulder. He squeezed hard enough so that it wasn't a friendly gesture.

"And maybe you should mind your own damn business." He hated that his words were slurred, but there wasn't much he could do about it. He also knew the other man was right, but he wouldn't give him the satisfaction of putting his drink down. If he wanted to finish the entire bottle of scotch, he would.

John grabbed his glass and tossed it into the ocean, then gave him a look that dared him to argue. Despite the urge to pummel the other man, Patrick knew it would be a mistake. John's black eyes were soulless. Every time they made eye contact, Patrick swore John could see inside him. He wouldn't admit it aloud, but the other man scared him shitless. John had been working for his father the past two years and he'd only seen him in action once.

It wasn't pretty.

"Let's go over this one more time," John said.

"Why? We've—"

"It's necessary. Now listen."

Patrick grunted an acknowledgement. They weren't letting him go with them, so what did he care?

"At dusk, we're taking the zodiac about a half mile down from their house. We should be back in an hour. Two hours tops. If we're not, you leave and I'll contact your father within a week. I don't want you hanging around inviting questions from anyone. Think you can remember that?"

"Yeah, I got it," he muttered. "Are you sure two men is enough?"

The other man snorted and stood, dismissing his question. Hell, Patrick doubted John even needed the other man at all. He was probably taking him to appease Patrick's father.

He laid his head back and groaned. They were still a couple hours away from Cuba and he was close to puking or passing out. The ride had been smooth so far, but a swell could come up at a moment's notice and his stomach would roil.

He wasn't even sure that bitch would be there. The information they'd received had been scanty, but a couple dock workers at the marina in Key West had confirmed she'd left the day before. Combined with his father's information, wherever that had come from, it appeared as if the bitch been hired by a wealthy family in Miami to do freelance work in Cuba.

At least they weren't on United States soil anymore. Another sign from the fates.

Chapter 5

Mac grabbed a beer from his fridge then walked out onto his lanai. The sound of the ocean normally soothed him. Not tonight though. He missed Hope. She traveled all over the world, but this time was different. That voice in the back of his head he rarely ignored had been whispering to him that something was wrong. He hadn't done an extensive check on the people who hired her since her agent had recommended them and hell, because he never had before. She was an adult and he didn't interfere in her work. The family that had hired her made money in coffee, donated to charity, and didn't make many social appearances. Almost none in fact, except the father.

His portable phone rang and after a glance at the caller ID, he answered. The area code was from DC. "Hello?"

"Mac, its Howard."

Howard Bishop, Deputy Director of the FBI's Washington DC division, didn't call unless it was important. Or if he needed a favor. "I don't think I'm going to like this."

Howard snorted. "There have been some people asking questions about Hope. Important people."

He pushed up from his sitting position, beer

forgotten. "Who?"

"Luke Romanov, for starters."

Mac nodded as some of his tension ebbed. It made sense. The man worked with the family who had hired her. It was only natural they'd want to check her out. "What's the big deal?"

"He ran an initial check before meeting her, but after they met he called a friend of his to run an extensive, off-the-record check."

"Who's his friend?"

"He works for me, and he's not going to help him. I made sure of it." Howard's answer was curt.

"You're sure?"

"As sure as I can be. That's only part of the reason I called. Another man, Richard Taylor, has been looking into her." His words deadpanned.

"Why does that name sound familiar?"

"He's old money, but you probably recognize him because he's made a killing in biotechnology in the past ten years."

"Why would he be interested in Hope?" Silence. Mac's grip on the phone tightened. "Don't hold out on me Howard. I want answers."

His friend sighed. "What I'm about to tell you is classified, and I don't want you flying off the handle before I've finished. Okay?"

"Fine."

"I can't tell you why, but we've been watching Richard Taylor for the past two years. His son is a real loser and...shit Mac, I'm just going to say it. He's put out a hit on Hope."

He heard the words, but couldn't believe they were true. "What?" He stood, sending the cheap plastic chair flying as his surroundings funneled out.

"Don't worry about it." Howard's voice was provokingly calm.

"What the hell do you mean, don't worry about it?" That was like telling him he had terminal cancer, but not to worry. He stormed into the house. The sliding glass door rattled behind him. He was going to be in Cuba by nightfall.

"I told you to let me finish. I've got a man on the inside."

Mac paused with a T-shirt hovering over his opened suitcase. "What does that mean?" His heartbeat slowed, but only by a fraction.

"I can't go into detail, and we don't even know why Taylor is after her. My contact couldn't get that much information out of him. The only thing we do know is he wants her dead. Immediately."

"Tell me again why I shouldn't be doing anything about this?" His hand balled into a tight fist around the shirt, wishing it was Richard Taylor's neck. Whoever he was.

"Because you'll blow my man's cover and ruin one of our biggest undercover operations." Howard's voice rose a fraction.

"I don't know about this," Mac muttered.

"Don't do anything stupid." When Mac didn't respond Howard pushed. "I want to hear you say it Mac."

Against his better judgment Mac relented. "I won't do anything stupid." That didn't mean he was going to sit by idly and do nothing.

"Good because there's more." His friend sighed again, a tiresome sound.

More? Nothing could be worse than what he'd already told him. "Lay it on me."

"I'm sending you an email with old articles and pictures of the Santiagos."

"Why should I care about them? Are they part of the reason this guy is after Hope?"

49

"Just check out what I'm sending you. With different people asking about Hope, I only checked them out to be thorough. Didn't want any surprises later on. I think you might find the key to Hope's past with them...If only we'd known all this years ago." He sighed and Mac could feel his insides shredding to ribbons.

Mac fired up his laptop as the other man talked. He wasn't sure what to expect, but he'd known Howard since Vietnam. They'd spent a year in a POW camp together. In all the years he'd known him, he'd never heard the other man sound unsure of himself. If it hadn't been for his friend, he wouldn't have been able to forge a new identity for Hope. They both owed each other in different ways, though Mac could never repay Howard. He might have saved Howard's life, but Howard had given him the gift of Hope.

"Have you pulled it up yet?"

"Give me a sec...almost there." Thank God for fast access internet. He scanned the message and uploaded the first attachment. His throat clenched. "Shit."

"That's what I thought you'd say."

"I'll call you back." Unable to say more, he hung up then opened up the rest of the attachments.

Articles and pictures dating back twenty-two years popped up. After a while he just scanned the headlines. *Parents of Missing Girl Ask for Closure, Wealthy Family Offers Reward for Any Information*...when he got to a current picture of the Santiagos, he thought his heart would give out. He couldn't believe what he was seeing.

The pixilation of the photo was grainy, taken through a telephoto lens if he had to guess. But the younger of the two women, the daughter, looked like Hope. Too much so for it to be a coincidence that they'd hired her.

Too many questions burned inside him. Hope said she'd grown up in foster care and he had believed her. No, he *still* believed her. She'd told him more than once she couldn't remember most of her childhood, just the years in foster care and...after. For years, she'd kept a journal next to her nightstand to record dreams, but she'd given that up long ago. He rubbed a hand over his face and finished packing his suitcase. He might not be leaving now, but he had a feeling that Hope would need him soon and he planned to be ready.

* * * * *

Hope let the shower jets massage her aching shoulders and back. She was used to harder work with her underwater dives, but she'd been in the sun all day and was feeling unusually burned out. She supposed it was because of the nightmare. Whatever it was, a feeling of dread hung over her head that she couldn't quite shake.

She could have finished a few hours ago, but in an effort to avoid Luke and the uncomfortable emotions he evoked, she'd taken about four hundred extra pictures. At least Mrs. Santiago would have a lot of prints to choose from. That was the reason she was here in the first place. Not to ogle over Luke's ripped stomach and very kissable chest. While his body was certainly hot, that's not what drew her to him.

The fact that he'd stayed in her room all night to make sure she was okay had totally taken her off guard. It had been sweet and at odds with what she'd expected from him.

When the water turned tepid she forced herself to get out. The small circular window in the bathroom told her it was near dusk and her stomach was growling embarrassingly loud. She pulled her damp hair into a low twist and changed into a lavender dress with Grecian flutter sleeves. She found Luke in the kitchen standing next to the stove, dicing green peppers.

"A man who cooks. I'm impressed." She tried to keep her tone casual, hoping her attitude would prevent him from mentioning anything about the night before.

He shot her a quick glance before pushing the peppers to the side. "I don't have anyone to cook for me so it was either learn or starve...or more likely live on takeout. What about you?" he asked as he pulled mushrooms and zucchini from the fridge.

"I've been cooking since I was ten." The truth was she'd had to learn. At age ten, she'd been placed in a home run by an elderly woman. Looking back, she realized the woman had been in the beginning stages of dementia, but the state hadn't cared. No one had. Like Luke said, she had to learn or she and the two younger girls living with her would have starved.

"Do you want to help?" he asked as he chopped the zucchini.

"Sure, where's Zara?" She didn't mind cooking, but she wondered where the eccentric older woman was. It would be nice to have a little barrier between her and Luke.

"I thought I told you. She's on her way back to Jamaica. She was only here to help get the house ready." He didn't look up as he spoke.

"Oh...right." Her stomach did an annoying little flip. They were alone. Not that it mattered. She was a consummate professional. Or at least that's what she kept telling herself. So why did her stomach tighten with need when she looked at him? And why did she keep envisioning what it would be like to be tangled between the sheets with him. Hell, who needed sheets or a bed when there was a kitchen table right here? Gritting her teeth, she mentally shook herself. She'd never had a runaway libido before, but Luke made her want so bad she ached.

Rolling her shoulders, she pushed down those

thoughts. "Is it all right if we eat in here, then? That dining room is so formal." *And intimate.*

"Definitely. I don't know why she insisted we eat in there last night." He chuckled and tossed vegetables in the frying pan.

She grabbed lettuce and other foodstuff and began to prepare a large salad. Out of the corner of her eye, she watched Luke move around the kitchen. He was dressed casually in dark jeans and an olive green polo shirt.

With deft hands, he diced vegetables, then grabbed a new knife and started slicing up fresh fish. She wondered if he often cooked for other women, then dismissed the thought as a surprising jolt of jealousy surged through her. It didn't matter.

She doubted he realized it, but he hummed an off-key ballad that had a hauntingly familiar sound. As if he knew she was staring at him, he glanced over from where he stood at the counter. She froze as his dark gaze swept over her. His look wasn't blatantly sexual, but there was no doubt in her mind that he was aware of her. Very aware. She wondered if he was even aware of the way he was watching her. Clearing her throat, she turned and began setting the table. She just wanted to eat and get the hell away from him.

He probably wouldn't do anything about it and that was just as well because she certainly wasn't going to make a move on him. It wasn't in her nature. Hell, she couldn't remember the last time she'd been on a date. And getting involved with someone she worked with was a definite no.

"What's that you're humming?"

"It's an old Russian folk song. I don't know why it's stuck in my head." He shook his head and returned to what he was doing.

"You don't have an accent, but you are Russian right?"

He nodded. "Yes. My parents immigrated before I was born."

"Any brothers or sisters?"

"No."

He was an only child just like her. She started to comment when the lights went out. Her heart stuttered. It wasn't raining or storming, but she also didn't know how well electricity in this region held up. "Is this normal?" she asked.

The two oversized kitchen windows let in a few muted streams of light. Dark reddish hues covered the patch of visible sky, and she could barely make out the shadows in the kitchen. Luke moved across the room with a liquid grace that surprised her. He put a finger over her mouth.

Instantly she tensed. If he was worried, she should be, too. She grabbed a knife off the kitchen table. In the dark Luke nodded so she knew she'd done the right thing. He motioned that she should follow him.

He squeezed her free hand and they quietly exited the kitchen. Feeling along the wall, they crept toward the stairs at the front of the house. Earlier, she'd seen the outline of a gun under the back of his shirt so she wasn't sure what he was doing since he already had a weapon. Her first instinct was to run out the back door instead of being trapped in this house, but she trusted him enough to follow.

She'd taken many self-defense classes over the years, but having that knife added another sense of security.

A thud sounded from behind them. Luke quickened his movements and she had no choice but to follow. When they made it to the stairs, he pulled out his gun, but kept her near his side. The carpeting muted their movements as they hurried toward his room.

Once inside he slipped the lock into place and pulled a flashlight from the bureau. Enough light filtered through his window that she could make out his movements, but it was growing darker by the second. She hated feeling like a spectator. After years of therapy and self-defense training, she couldn't sit on the sidelines.

Keeping her movements slow, she walked up to Luke and pulled his head down to her so that his ear was inches from her mouth. "What's going on?"

"I don't know. Break-ins aren't common, but I'm not taking a chance with you here. There's a jeep in the covered shed behind the rose garden. I needed to get the keys," he whispered back into her ear.

Okay, so they were leaving. That was fine with her. She hated that she might lose all her camera equipment but she wasn't stupid enough to argue.

He handed her his gun and slipped a cell phone into his back pocket, then grabbed another gun and a set of keys. She left the knife on the bed. Briefly she wondered if it was even legal for him to have a gun with him, then quickly discarded the thought. To hell with legalities.

A loud crash sounded downstairs from the kitchen, like someone had run into a chair or table. Luke motioned that he was going out first. He swept the hallway with his gun before motioning that she should follow. She noted he didn't turn the flashlight on.

Trying to keep her breathing as normal and quiet as possible, she felt along the wall. They passed her room and were almost to the edge of the stairs when the hair on the back of her neck raised. Warning tingles snaked down her spine. Before she could motion to Luke that something was off, a pair of steely arms wrapped around her upper body.

Body odor and tobacco assaulted her senses. The smell was disgustingly familiar, and a rage buried deep inside unleashed her animalistic side.

She didn't think. She reacted. Being small had

advantages. In a few swift movements, she shoved her arms outward at the same time she bent her knees to escape the embrace. Her gun dropped, but it didn't matter. In calculated, fluid movements, she pivoted and prayed her elbow connected with something. The crunch of bone reverberated through the air. A man screamed obscenities. She wasn't finished, though.

She could feel Luke behind her, but she ignored him.

The intruder's shadow was visible enough now that she was facing him, so she advanced. It wasn't the smartest thing she'd ever done, but something primal took over and she just acted. She kicked at one of his knees and was perversely pleased when he crumpled to the floor, howling in pain.

"Run!" Luke shouted.

He jerked her back and out of the way, then yelled at her again to get the jeep. As he lunged for the other man, he threw something over his shoulder toward her. Keys clattered to the floor. Heart racing, she felt around in the semi-darkness for a few seconds before her fingers clasped around the jagged metal.

She wanted to stay and help but had no doubts about Luke's ability to defend them. Not to mention his order to retrieve their getaway vehicle. If there was more than one person in the house she and Luke needed a way to escape. Grunts and the sound of fighting trailed behind her and she sent up a silent prayer for Luke.

She raced down the stairs but paused when the lights flooded back on. Beads of sweat ran down her back and face. She had no idea why the lights were back on, but she assumed it wasn't good. She flung open the front door, and all the air whooshed from her lungs.

A blond-haired man dressed in all black stood on the porch. He had a gun pointed directly at her face. "Back inside now."

She did as he said, but refused to turn her back to

him. When they were back in the foyer and the front door was closed, he spoke again. "Where's your friend?"

"Long gone."

The noises and grunts from upstairs proved her a liar. *Damn!*

He lifted a sandy eyebrow mockingly. Without turning his head he shouted, "Luke, you might want to get down here."

Her heart sped up. Did Luke know this man? Her confusion must have shown because he continued. "I know who you are too, Hope."

Alternating rushes of hot and cold snaked down her spine. She wiped clammy palms on her dress. Seconds later Luke came down the stairs with a groaning man in front of him. With a steady hand, Luke held a gun to his head. When Luke saw the other man and Hope, his eyes narrowed at her. Did he actually think she knew who this guy was? The man was pointing a gun at her for God's sake.

She glanced back at the guy and realized he hadn't taken his eyes off her. Smart man.

"Let him go." The stranger with the gun had a surprisingly even voice. As if this was something he did every day.

For all she knew, he did.

The bearded man in front of Luke stumbled down the stairs, muttering under his breath, but he didn't look pissed. Just annoyed. She glanced back and forth between Luke and the blond man holding the gun. Inside, her adrenaline pumped at lightning speed.

When Luke and his prisoner got to the bottom of the stairs, Luke jerked the man by the collar up against his body, using him as a shield. Looked like he wasn't going to follow the other guy's directives and let his captive go. *Good.*

That's when she realized the other man's hands were

secured behind his back with some kind of plastic flex-cuffs. Keeping his weapon trained on the man with the gun, Luke cautiously walked backward toward Hope.

"Who are you and what the hell do you want?" Luke demanded as he came to stand near Hope. Actually, he stood more in front of her than beside her, shielding her. His neck muscles corded tightly, his shoulders were tense, and she could practically feel the adrenaline rolling off him. Despite the crazy situation, some small part of her melted because he was using his body to block hers.

"I want you two to disappear for three days." The blond man spoke calmly.

"What?" they asked in unison.

Before he could answer, the man Luke held in a death grip grunted in pain. From her position she could see trickles of blood streaming down his face. "Damn it, you should have warned me she knew kung fu or whatever the hell that was."

She almost felt bad for him. But not quite.

The blond man ignored his partner as he sheathed his gun. "For three days you need to be invisible. Understand?"

Hope allowed a small measure of relief to course through her as the man's weapon disappeared.

"Who are you?" she asked, and couldn't stop the rising pitch of her voice. Normally she handled stressful situations well, but today she felt her sanity pull thin. Probably had something to do with the gun that had just been pointed at her *face*.

"That's not important. What is important, is that a very powerful man wants you dead." He spoke directly to her, with a pointed stare, as if she should have a clue as to what he was talking about.

"Her?" Luke demanded.

"Me? Who wants me dead?" After her late night

phone calls, she had a small guess, but she didn't have a name to go with the face. Her throat tightened at the thought that *he* had somehow found her. The man from her nightmares. And what, he'd sent people to kill her? Now this guy was letting her go instead? Nothing made sense. Her temple throbbed as a hundred questions assaulted her.

The man paused and she guessed he was deciding how much he could tell them. Eventually he spoke. "A man named Richard Taylor."

The name wasn't familiar. She gnawed on her bottom lip. Maybe this was the break she'd been waiting for since she was fifteen. Maybe she could finally find peace or at least closure.

"Three days is all I need, then you'll never have to worry about Richard Taylor again. You've got twenty minutes to grab what you need and get out of here. Don't take that yacht. You're supposed to be dead."

"Fine." Luke nodded then shoved his prisoner forward.

Without pause, the two men walked out the front door. They didn't even stop to cut his cuffs off.

Luke stepped forward as if he was having second thoughts about letting them go, but Hope grabbed his arm. If they'd wanted them dead, they would be. The stranger's intentions might not be clear, but his order was concise. They needed to get out of there.

When they were gone, Luke turned toward her, his voice accusing. "I thought you were a photographer."

The hair on the back of her neck rose and she yanked her hand away. "I am. And I don't like your tone."

"Why would someone put out a hit on a photographer?" His eyes narrowed.

"Do you really want to worry about that now?" She rolled her eyes to cover her very real fear and started for the stairs. She stood at the bottom of the stairwell, waiting for him to make a decision. As much as she wanted to scream in frustration about what was happening, she couldn't. They needed to keep a level head and get out of the house in case those two guys changed their minds and came back.

It was obvious Luke was torn between grilling her and getting out of there. "Fine, but this isn't over."

* * * * *

Hope held on to the fraying straps that secured her against the side of the hollowed out Cessna. When Luke said they'd be flying to Jamaica, she'd expected a small two-seater plane. She hadn't expected to be strapped into a cargo hull sharing the trip with crates of coconuts, pineapples, and what she was fairly sure was marijuana.

Directly across from her on the other side of the plane, Luke was strapped in, too. His eyes were closed, but she was almost certain he wasn't asleep. He'd barely said two words as they'd grabbed their stuff and had only spoken directly to her when she'd asked a question. Even if she'd wanted to talk to him, she could barely hear herself think above the engine. Apparently the owner of the plane didn't see any reason to add insulation or sound-proofing. Then again, they probably didn't transport people very often.

Luke seemed to have a plan and since her mind was still reeling, she wasn't going to fight him. As soon as they landed, she needed internet access. If someone had enough money to hire a killer, then there was a good chance they were well-known enough to be on the internet.

The plane dipped suddenly and Luke's eyes flew open. They made eye contact, but just as quickly he averted his eyes to the front of the plane. He was ignoring her and that just pissed her off. He had no right to be angry at her when she'd done nothing wrong.

As the plane twisted violently, her stomach pitched with nausea. Everything not strapped down shifted. Crates and random fruit rolled around the interior. When the plane twisted again, she yelped as something struck her head. Before she had a chance to absorb the pain, blackness engulfed her.

Chapter 6

The man everyone called John pulled out one of his throw away cell phones and dialed a familiar number as he and his partner hiked down the deserted beach.

His boss picked up on the second ring. "Bishop, here."

"It's done." He didn't identify himself and didn't even consider going into details over an unsecured line.

"You're sure?"

"Yes. We have three days." He glanced around, even though it was nearly pitch black. Clouds covered the moon and stars, veiling their existence.

"Where are they?"

"They won't cause any trouble until the deal is done. Trust me." If time had allowed, they would have taken Hope and Luke into protective custody and placed them in a safe house. But these weren't normal circumstances, and he couldn't risk a leak or trust anyone but himself.

He'd been working for Richard Taylor for two years. This job had cost him his marriage, his life. One way or another, he was bringing that bastard down.

"Call me when you have the location of the meet," Bishop said.

"Done." He disconnected.

"What did the boss man say?" Sanders asked as they

neared the waiting zodiac.

"Just to call him when we have more details about the big meeting." The salty water drenched them as they waded in.

His partner nodded, and they both pushed the small boat into the waves before jumping in. "Why do you think Richard wanted her dead? She didn't even know him."

"Don't know." He had a few guesses, but Taylor hadn't seen fit to tell him why the girl needed to die. Just that she did. Considering he'd sent that weasel son of his with them, he could make an educated assumption.

Now that he'd proved himself, John had no doubt he and Sanders would be included in Richard's more intimate dealings. Until recently he'd been nothing more than hired muscle. Things would drastically change after tonight. Or at least he hoped they would. If not, he'd wasted two years.

"Do you really trust them to stay out of sight for three days?"

He nodded. "Luke Romanov isn't an idiot." He'd reviewed the other man's file and was satisfied he'd be astute enough to listen. Luke had former military experience, and he ran a million-dollar security company. By now, he'd probably guessed they worked for the government.

"You think Richard will include us in the deal now?" Sanders' voice was barely audible over the engine and ocean waves.

He nodded and said a silent prayer he was right. "He'd better or we've wasted two years."

Once they made it back to the yacht, Patrick was passed out. No surprise there. Instead of waking him, John called Patrick's father, who'd demanded proof. John had counted on that, so he sent Richard Taylor a picture of two bodies charred beyond recognition to an encrypted phone.

Now if he could just wrap up this undercover job, he could go back to his life.

What was left of it.

* * * * *

Hope opened her eyes and groaned. Light filtered in through a sliding glass door, bathing her in warmth. She sat up and immediately clutched the back of her head. After a few moments, the pain abated, so she pushed the unfamiliar palm tree covered comforter off and ventured out of bed. She shivered when her feet hit the cool tile floor. After a quick glance around, she guessed she was in a villa or a cottage. No personal items lay on the shelves or dresser and the room had a hotel feel to it.

She padded across the floor toward the glass door and drew back the sheer white curtain. In cargo shorts and a plain brown T-shirt, Luke stood with his back to her, facing the aquamarine water and talking on his cell phone. Without announcing her presence, she walked outside, savoring the feel of the sun-warmed grass underneath her feet.

"I'll call you when I know more," he growled before flipping his phone shut.

"Uh, hi." She held up a hand, trying to block the sun and get his attention.

He swiveled and his expression softened instantly. "Hey, how are you feeling?" Before she could answer, he continued. "Here, sit." With a gentleness she hadn't expected, he led her to one of the lounge chairs.

"Where are we?"

"A friend is letting us stay here. We're on the northern coast of Jamaica. Right on Discovery Bay." He motioned behind him to the still waters of the bay, his eyes never leaving hers.

She wasn't sure what it was, but something had changed in him. And that's when it hit her. She was wearing a pair of light blue cotton pajama pants and a matching tank top. Both of which, she hadn't put on herself. She could feel the heat slowly creep up her neck and cheeks. "Did you dress me?"

He sat on the edge of the chair. "Yes, but are you sure you're okay?" Worry lines etched around his dark eyes.

"I think so. What happened?" He didn't even seem fazed that he'd dressed her. She got all hot and bothered at the sight of him without a shirt on and he didn't care that he'd seen her naked. Ouch.

"You were hit by a coconut."

When he said coconut, she remembered the plane and the jostling and…"I remember now."

"You'll probably be sore today. You might have a concussion, but I doubt it. I woke you up a few times and you were fine."

"You did?" Her memory was fuzzy around the edges.

"You don't remember?" His frown deepened as he stared at her.

Now that he said something she had vague snatches of him sitting next to her on a bed, rubbing her hair back from her face and saying gentle words. "Kind of."

"Listen, earlier, I'm sorry if I accused you—"

"It's fine. Do you have a computer?" She was sure he had questions, but chances were she couldn't answer any of them, and she needed to look up Richard Taylor.

"Yes, and I'm already one step ahead of you." He shifted along the seat, moving a few inches closer.

She swallowed hard as his intoxicating, spicy scent twined around her. Probably not what she should be focusing on. "You are?"

"I've pulled up everything I could find on him, but you need to eat, first."

She didn't like people ordering her around, but his 'order' sounded more like a plea so she didn't argue. Besides, her stomach was growling.

He stood and held out a hand to help her to her feet. Normally standing didn't require effort, but her body felt as if it had been through a blender. As they walked across the perfectly manicured lawn, she asked, "Why are you being so nice?"

"Guilt." His answer was quick. Maybe he'd been expecting her question.

"Oh."

"I was an ass. You were just as surprised by that attack as I was, but I was too stubborn to admit it. I was taken off guard…and that rarely happens."

She was silent as he held open the door leading to the kitchen.

He continued, almost reluctantly. "And, I was embarrassed."

Her head whipped up. "Why?"

"I should have protected you better. It's what I do for a living," he muttered as faint redness crept up his neck.

"No one could have predicted what happened. Hell, I still don't believe what happened and I was there." She placed a light hand on his arm. When his muscles flexed under her grasp, she immediately let go.

"We'll figure it out. Apparently we've got three days to kill." He popped two bagel halves in the toaster, and she took a seat at the glass-top kitchen table.

"Who were you talking to earlier?"

He pulled cream cheese and jelly from the refrigerator as he answered. "My partner. He thinks we should come back to Miami."

"And you don't?" She'd wondered what his plan was. She couldn't blame him for contacting his partner because she planned to contact Mac as soon as she figured out a few more things.

"No. I was pissed at first–well, I'm still pissed—but the more I think about it, I think those guys work for the government. And I think we should do exactly as they said. We're supposed to be gone for a couple weeks anyway so no one is going to miss us. I bet in three days we're going to see Richard Taylor on the news for a big bust of some kind."

"Wait a minute, when you say government, you mean our government?" She couldn't keep the disbelief out of her voice.

He shrugged as he pulled out plates and utensils. "They knew too much about us and they let us go. Once we figure out who Richard Taylor is, I think we'll have our answers."

"What happens if we don't hear anything in three days?"

"Then we head back to Florida and we'll figure something out. No matter what, I'll make sure you have protection."

She stared out one of the windows and digested his words. Palm trees swayed with the wind, but she forced herself to look away. She was getting nauseous. The bagels popped from the toaster and she jumped in her seat.

"Cream cheese?" He placed a plate in front of her and sat across the table with his own.

She nodded, but stopped him when he started smoothing cream cheese on her bread. "I can get it." He handed it to her, but she didn't miss the worried expression in his dark eyes. "I'm fine, I promise. I think I liked you better when you were angry at me." She smiled, hoping he'd realize she was joking, but all she received in return was a frown.

Hope wouldn't admit it aloud, but she liked the change in him. Mac and Frank were the only men who fussed over her. Actually, they were the only men in her life she allowed to get close to her. Thanks to years of therapy she might have gotten over her fear of sex, but that didn't mean she dated with frequency.

Or at all, really. Men were too much hassle, and sex wasn't all that great. Although she knew it had to be. People wouldn't make such a big deal about it if there wasn't more to it than what she'd experienced.

Neither said anything while they ate, but as soon as they finished, she was ready to start researching. After he placed both their plates in the sink she was practically jumping up and down. At least internally.

"Can I look at your computer now?" she asked.

Nodding, he disappeared through the open entryway. The whole house appeared to be tiled, and his feet squeaked along the floor. Seconds later he was back with his laptop. He plugged it in and placed it on the table.

"You've been busy," she commented as she scrolled through different articles he'd marked as favorites. Richard Taylor even had his own Wikipedia article. Apparently biotechnology was very lucrative. Why would he have an interest in her though?

"And you don't recognize him?" Luke hovered behind her, watching the screen as she scrolled.

She shook her head. "Not even a little bit. None of this makes sense. Are you sure this is the right Richard Taylor?"

"He's the only one who came up who lives near—" His phone rang, cutting him off. "That's my partner. I need to take this."

She nodded without glancing at him. She was curious about his business partner since he hadn't mentioned one, but nothing could stop her from what she was doing. The thud of the door behind her told her she was alone. Clicking on the family link in the Wikipedia article she hoped to garner more background. "Wife dead, son…" She stopped scrolling at the face on the screen.

Despite the meal she'd just had, a hollow feeling settled in her gut. After years of wondering and years of recurring nightmares she finally had a name and face to the man who had changed her life. A face to the man who had ripped away what little childhood she had left.

Bile rose in her throat. She wanted to run to the private bathroom attached to her bedroom but knew she'd never make it. She stumbled blindly toward the sink, and emptied the contents of her stomach until she was dry heaving. Still hunched over the sink she clutched the counter with one hand and turned on the faucet, hoping to hide the evidence. She couldn't handle more questions from Luke. He was biding his time before he asked more, and she couldn't deal with an onslaught. If he asked her anything now she was liable to break down and tell him everything.

She'd hate herself for it later.

She wished she *could* just tell Luke everything. He had a right to know why someone was after them, but if she told him, then she'd have to explain how she came to live with Mac. She wasn't ashamed of what had happened to her—not anymore—but she didn't want to put Mac in danger. He'd taken in a young, difficult teenager with a lot of baggage and had never made her feel unwanted. Over the years, no matter what, she'd known she was loved unconditionally. Something foreign in her experience. It had taken a long time, but she'd finally learned to cope with her past and to accept that Mac would always be there for her. She couldn't betray the one man who'd given her that gift.

Just as the last remnants disappeared down the drain, the door opened. Luke walked in and it looked like he had news, but a sharp unexpected wetness stung her eyes. Brushing past him, she fled to her room. She refused to cry in front of him.

After she shut the door behind herself, she pushed out a shaky breath and managed to contain her tears. She found her cell phone buried in one of her bags. After turning it on, she stared at it for a long moment before calling Mac. He needed to know what was going on. If someone was after her, then it was probable they knew who Mac was. She had no doubt he could take care of himself but he had a right to know he was in danger.

After pressing the first speed dial, she held her breath.

He answered on the first ring. "Hope! What's going on?"

She swallowed. Unless he was psychic, he couldn't already know she was in Jamaica. "Why do you sound so wired?"

"I've been trying to reach you for the past thirteen hours. Why hasn't your phone been on?" His words came out in a rush.

"I'm not exactly sure where to start." She fell back onto the bed and stared at the ceiling.

"The beginning is normally a good place," he said quietly.

Ten minutes later she'd spilled everything, including who Patrick Taylor was, the son of the man who'd put out a hit on her. Saying the words aloud twisted her gut, but it also gave her a sense of freedom. And in a weird way, closure. Maybe not completely, but putting a name to his face still helped. "So, what do you think?"

"For starters, the man who let you go wasn't lying. He does work for our government. He's undercover."

She sat upright in bed. "How could you possibly know that?"

"It's part of the reason I've been so worried about you. Bishop called and told me Richard Taylor put out a hit on you, but that he had a man on the inside who wouldn't let anything happen to you. I didn't understand why a stranger would want you dead. It didn't make sense until...until now." His voice broke on the last syllable.

Ah, the infamous Bishop. It seemed the man knew everything about everything. "Don't do anything stupid," she warned.

"What's that supposed to mean?" By his subdued tone, she guessed he knew exactly what she meant.

"You know precisely what it means. Just because we know who...it doesn't mean you have liberty to do *anything*." The thought of him behind bars or worse because of her was something she couldn't have hanging on her conscience. Life without Mac was unimaginable.

When he didn't answer, she continued. "I want you to promise. At least for right now. Come on Mac, you're my only family. What would I do without you?" If she had to play the guilt card she would.

"Fine." He sighed the word.

"And you have to promise you won't tell Frank." She knew Mac. He'd find a loophole to his promise if he wanted.

"Damn it Hope, I promise." It came out as a growl.

He might not be happy about it, but she knew he'd never lie to her. "Okay, is there anything else your friend told you I should know about?"

"No," he said *almost* immediately. The pause was slight, but enough that she caught it.

Her head hurt though and she didn't feel like playing a game of twenty questions. Because if Mac didn't want to tell her something it would be hell getting him to open up. Assuming he would at all. "Okay, I've got my cell phone on now so you can reach me anytime."

After they disconnected she brushed her teeth and got in the shower in an effort to clear her head. She'd have to face Luke eventually, but she needed time.

* * * * *

Luke clenched his fists at his sides. The urge to follow after Hope clawed at him, but he stayed where he was in an effort to give her privacy. He'd seen her get sick through the kitchen window, but hadn't wanted to intrude. She wasn't the kind of woman to show weakness and while he respected that, she called to the most primitive, protective side of him. Whether it was because he thought she might be Anna, he didn't know. But he was pretty sure that had nothing to do with it.

Last night he'd been more pissed at himself than the situation. He should have protected her. Then when that coconut had slammed against her head with a sickening thud, he'd lost ten years of his life. He'd have given his left nut to trade places with her in that instant. She'd hung there looking so helpless and there hadn't been a damn thing he could do about it until they landed. And then to endure the torture of having to undress her. He'd tried to ignore her smooth, lean body but it had been damn near impossible to avoid looking at her the entire time. He rubbed a hand over his face as if he could somehow erase the memory of what she'd looked like. Unfortunately he couldn't.

The woman might look like his childhood friend, but Maria had never made him feel the way Hope did. She was getting under his skin in a bad way and there wasn't a damn thing he could do about it. He wasn't sure he wanted to.

Sighing, Luke pulled up his computer's history. The screen flashed to life, but instead of a picture of Richard Taylor, he found a picture of the man's son. He tapped his finger against the wireless mouse as he tried to put together the disjointed puzzle pieces in his head.

Hope was telling the truth about not knowing Richard Taylor. He was almost sure of it. Unless she led a double life as an actress, she'd been just as confused as he had. As he stared at Patrick Taylor's picture, a thought entered his mind. He pulled out his phone and hit redial.

"Miss me already?" Kyle Vargas, his smart-ass partner answered on the first ring.

"Do me a favor and see if you can run Patrick Taylor's records."

"That's the son, right?"

"Yeah."

"No problem. Why? Should I be looking for anything specific?"

"Just a hunch I have. Find out where he went to college. See if he had any incidents there and see if he's got a rap sheet."

"I'll call you as soon as I find anything."

After they disconnected, Luke knocked on Hope's door. If she wanted to be alone, fine. He had to make sure she wasn't sick from her head injury, though. "Hope? Are you okay?"

"I'm fine. Just resting."

"Are you sure? I could—"

"I said I'm fine!"

He dropped his arm to his side, sighed, cleaned up the kitchen, and tried to think about anything but Hope.

So far, he'd had Kyle increase the Santiagos' security just in case this had anything to do with them. He doubted it did, but he wasn't taking any chances. He couldn't call anyone other than his partner because he was supposed to be invisible, aka dead, for the next three days. Sonja would probably go crazy not being able to contact him, but that's the way it had to be.

After two hours and the tenth glance at his watch, he decided to knock on Hope's door. He stopped when his cell phone buzzed. It was his partner again. "Hey."

"I just emailed you a list of Patrick Taylor's *indiscretions*. This guy's a real winner." Kyle's voice was grim.

"All right, give me a second. I need to pull up my account." He moved back to the kitchen table.

"Okay. By the way, Maria and Sonja called and they're pissed they can't get a hold of you. I told them you were out of cell range."

He leaned back in the cushioned chair as his computer flared back to life. "They can deal. I'll be back by Friday or Saturday." If they didn't have any news after three days, he'd think about giving it another two before taking matters into his own hands. They could only pretend to be dead for so long and he wasn't letting anything happen to Hope.

"I think I managed to hold them off for a couple days."

"Good." In case anyone was listening to the Santiagos' calls, the official story was that he wasn't reachable by phone. And Kyle was only calling him from a secure location. He didn't think Richard Taylor would look into their deaths once the man he'd hired gave him proof. And he had no doubt that man had concocted some sort of proof. He was obviously a professional.

"Have you pulled up your email yet?"

"It's coming up right now." He opened the attachment and scrolled down the list of Taylor's indiscretions. After he got to the second page, he wanted to put his fist through Patrick Taylor's face. "You weren't kidding," he muttered.

"Call me if it's important, but if not, I won't bother you until Thursday."

They disconnected, and Luke tried to digest the expansive report Kyle had put together. Taylor's father had covered up—meaning paid off—a couple women Patrick assaulted in college. He'd been charged with sexual assault on a minor a few times, but the charges never stuck. Which probably meant his father had paid those families off, too.

When he got to the third page, the door to Hope's bedroom creaked open so he quickly shut down his email. He turned to face her, and it felt like a knife embedded in his chest. Her eyes were slightly puffy and red. It wasn't hard to figure out the rest. Looked like his hunch was right.

He opened his mouth to ask what had happened with her and Patrick Taylor, but the vulnerable look in her pale eyes wouldn't allow him. Instead he asked, "Do you want to take advantage of the weather and go swimming?"

The relief in her eyes was so palpable his gut twisted. He wanted nothing more than to comfort her. For the time being he'd hold off on his questions. He wouldn't be the cause of her pain.

Chapter 7

"Let me change." Hope's lips curved into a smile. Once again she disappeared into her room.

After changing into swim trunks, Luke left his phone, but brought two towels. He kept a gun wrapped in one and waited in the backyard. They were on a private beach, so he wasn't worried about anyone stealing or discovering it. It was his just-in-case weapon.

The thought of being without any outside communication for the next three days was strange, but he couldn't think of one other person he'd rather spend those days with.

That thought alone unsettled him. He was just getting to know Hope. He *wanted* to know everything about her, but she seemed determined to keep him at arm's length.

A few minutes later she walked out the sliding glass door connected to her room wearing a blue one-piece bathing suit, carrying two disposable cameras and two underwater masks. His mouth went dry at the sight of her. Her suit covered everything, but the way the Lycra material clung to her curves had to be a sin. Looking at her made him think of pure sex. The suit molded perfectly to her softly rounded breasts and he could just see the outline of her nipples—

"You okay?" Her head cocked slightly to the side as she looked at him.

"What are those for?" he gestured to the cameras, knowing how stupid the question sounded, but he had to say something.

She tossed one to him as she walked up. "I thought it might be fun to take pictures."

"You're not going to bring one of your professional cameras?"

She shrugged as they walked toward the private sandy beach. "There isn't a reef so the pictures won't be that interesting, and honestly, I didn't feel like pulling all my gear out. I'm still trying to grasp..." She shook her head and sighed.

He could understand why she didn't want to think or work. Having someone try to kill you was definitely out of the ordinary for someone like her. It was out of the ordinary for him, too. At least now. Back in his military days he'd seen some action, but now he usually dealt with white collar criminals trying to rip off the Santiagos.

Not exactly riveting excitement.

To be honest, he was surprised she hadn't freaked out yet. Most women he dated got annoyed if they had to wait too long for the valet driver. Hope was under an insane amount of stress, yet she hadn't complained.

The grass sloped downward until they reached the beach. He dug his feet into the warm sand and tried to remember the last time he'd taken a vacation. Technically this wasn't a vacation, but he had nothing to do and no one to bother them for the next few days.

They laid their towels out in the sand, but he made sure to keep his gun covered. No need to worry her unnecessarily. He could practically see the gears turning in her head. Unless he'd completely misread the situation, she knew who was after her and why.

KATIE REUS

However, he couldn't figure out what her plan was. And he couldn't ask without admitting what he knew. Or thought he knew.

"How long has it been since you've taken a vacation?"

She glanced up at his question and laughed self-deprecatingly. "Is it sad that I can't remember?"

"Good, now I don't feel so pathetic," he said as he walked with her down to the ocean. She didn't seem as paranoid about her scars as before and he was relieved. He didn't give a shit about something like that. If anything, they made her more beautiful. Hell, he had a few scars of his own. He'd served four years in the Marines in Force Recon. Half his scars were from training alone.

A few ripples played across the clear water as they waded in. Except for a handful of sailboats dotting the bay, they were basically alone. Exactly like he wanted. The salty smell enveloped them the deeper they went.

He decided a few small questions couldn't hurt. If he gained her trust, she might open up to him. "Those were some pretty impressive moves last night."

Without glancing in his direction she waded deeper. "I've been studying aikido for over a decade."

Damn. "Do you have any idea why someone is after you?"

"No." She shook her head before completely submersing herself in the water. When she came back up, drops of water glistened off her eyelashes, face, and body. Her hardened nipples were visible through the sheer material of her suit and he tried to ignore his physical response. Not that it did any good. She was his living, breathing fantasy, and there wasn't a damn thing he could do about it. It wasn't even her physical appearance. No doubt she was smoking hot, but she looked just like his childhood friend. It was the way she

78

handled herself. In what should be one of the toughest situations she'd possibly ever faced, she'd handled herself like a pro.

That alone was sexy.

He mentally shook his head. He couldn't think about that. There were more important things at stake. "It's just strange that—"

With a wave of her hand, she interrupted him. "Can we just take a break from all this for a couple hours? My head hurts from thinking about everything and talking isn't making it better." Her pale blue eyes silently begged him.

When had he turned into such a pushover? "Sure. Just point and click right?" He held up the plastic-covered camera.

She waded near and held up hers. "Yep, just make sure you use a flash at all times."

"Why? It's the middle of the day."

"Water absorbs light at an alarming rate. Your suit will probably turn out almost black in the pictures." She motioned to his dark red swim trunks.

Something tickled his legs so he looked down. She did the same. A sea of tiny silver fish rushed past them.

A playful grin pulled at her lips. "Come on. Let's swim a little deeper."

Before he could respond, she put her mask in place and dove under, camera in hand. He followed suit, but barely kept pace with her. He kept in shape by running and occasionally swimming laps, but she was an exceptionally strong swimmer. If they were on land, he had no doubt he'd be a stronger runner, but in the water she was like a fish. Or a graceful mermaid. He had to return to the surface for air more than twice as fast as she did.

There wasn't a reef close by, but the colorful tropical fish and Hope in a bathing suit was enough entertainment for him. A huge sea turtle swam by, and he tried to take a few pictures, but forgot the flash. Yeah, he definitely wasn't cut out for this, but admired that Hope could do this for hours and days on end. She somehow managed to keep herself buoyed down and still take pictures of a school of fish. She must have sensed him watching her because she turned around and smiled. She waved, but her eyes widened suddenly and she frantically pointed behind him.

He turned and came face to face with a funny-looking fish. It was striped red, brown, and yellow, and looked like it had spines. Almost like a dragon. Maybe she wanted a picture. He pulled up his camera again, but before he could snap a picture, Hope's arm encircled his waist and yanked him backward. He tensed, but didn't fight her. Instead he joined in kicking backward.

Seconds later they resurfaced. He started to ask what was wrong, but she didn't give him a chance.

"Swim, now." Her voice held no room for argument.

He matched her stroke for stroke until they were sitting in shallow water by the shore. He was slightly panting but she was barely winded.

"What was that all about?" He took off his mask and tossed it behind him. It landed in the sand with a thump.

"That was a lion fish, and if it had stung you, your leg would have swelled and knotted up." She crossed her legs, then twisted water out of her hair.

"It didn't look dangerous." He ran a hand through his hair, trying to shake out the excess water.

Hope chuckled. "Trust me, you'd have been howling in pain if that thing had touched you. They're not native to these waters, but for some reason they've been migrating across the ocean. Worse, they don't have any natural enemies."

Being stung would have been icing on the cake for how their week was going. The only thing he knew to stay away from was sharks so he couldn't help but be impressed. "Uh, thanks then."

She laughed again and leaned over toward him. Surprised by her casual movements, he instinctively moved back. He wanted to get close to her, but every fiber in his body told him what could happen between them if he let her get too close. "What?"

"You've got seaweed stuck to your face." She reached out and her hand grazed his cheek. Her soft touch sent an electric jolt through his body.

Without thinking, he caught her wrist, encircling it with his fingers. Her eyes widened, but she didn't pull away. Her tongue darted out to moisten her lips as her eyes fell to his mouth. He watched her breathing slightly hitch as she brought her gaze back up to his. She was a hard woman to read but if her heart was pounding as loud as his, they were both in trouble. Neither said anything for a long moment. He could hear a few birds and a loud horn in the distance. Other than that, the sound of his heartbeat pounding in his ears overtook everything else. Including his ability to think rationally.

He knew what he was about to do was a mistake, but in the moment before their lips met, he couldn't think of one good reason why he should stop.

Luke was going to kiss her. Hope knew it. She also knew it was a mistake, but she didn't care. Her entire body was on fire just thinking about it. That had never happened before. Men usually affected her with disgust or indifference. Not this searing need to feel his body against hers. Over hers.

Consuming her.

The second their lips met, all coherent thought fled. His kiss was soft and gentle, not what she'd expected from a man like him. Everything else about him was hard and intense, but he kissed her like a man with all the time in the world. He tugged on her bottom lip gently, teasingly. All the air left her lungs and she had to remind herself to breathe. As their lips and tongues danced, so much tension ebbed from her body.

Without much warning, his hands strayed to her waist and he shifted her so that she straddled him. The feel of her inner thighs sliding against his outer legs created an interesting friction. And the pulsing between her legs...she shuddered.

He straightened his position so she clutched his shoulders for support. Her body was undergoing an assault of new sensations. With her eyes closed, everything seemed intensified tenfold. The sound of the ocean, the feel of his hands caressing down her sides, the aching between her legs. Luke trailed his hands higher until his fingers slid through her wet hair and pulled her closer. His grip wasn't rough or tight. Which gave her another sense of security.

He pulled his mouth away and her eyes flew open. Inches apart, their gazes clashed. His eyes filled with lust, she knew he wasn't going to stop. Not unless she told him to. He lifted his eyebrows in a silent question. *Did she want him to stop?* Unable to find her voice, she shook her head.

Something indefinable flashed in his eyes, but his head dipped and he raked his teeth over her neck before she could form any more thoughts. When his tongue flicked over her pulse point she jumped at the erotic gesture. Being on top of him gave her an advantage and made her feel almost powerful. More in control of the situation. Which was what she desperately needed.

She squeezed her legs together in a vain attempt to ease the growing ache. This was new to her. This growing need. She felt a little lightheaded, out of control. His mouth moved leisurely along her neck and collarbone as he tested her response. She arched her back closer to him, not exactly sure what she wanted, just that she needed him touching her. When she shifted her body, he rubbed a thumb over one of her hardened nipples.

It was over the stretchy material, not even on her bare body, but the effect was almost torturous. She jolted at the new sensations zinging through her body.

He paused and pulled his head back. One hand hovered on her bathing suit strap. "I want to see you."

This was all happening so fast. Too fast though? Other than Luke's piercing gaze, the sound of her heartbeat pounding in her ears was the only thing she was aware of.

Unsure of her own voice, she nodded. He pulled down the two straps of her suit, one at a time. The feel of them sliding down her arms made her shiver. And the possessive, appreciative way he stared at her did something strange to her stomach.

"You're perfect," he murmured against her neck as he kissed his way down to her breasts.

Her lower abdomen tightened when he rolled his tongue over a nipple. She was so close to finding release, she knew she wouldn't last much longer. He hadn't touched her anywhere else, and she was ready to combust. The juncture between her legs was incredibly wet. It made no sense, but her body was responding as if she'd been living in a convent for the past decade. In erotic little circles, he licked and teased her nipples with the same devotion he'd paid to her mouth and neck.

Her hands dug into his back as she tried to ground herself back in reality. It was useless. With each little flick she pushed closer and closer to orgasm.

When his hand moved between her legs, momentary panic threatened to settle, but he didn't attempt to move the material separating them. He simply rubbed over her clit through her bathing suit and simultaneously sucked hard on one breast. And she came. Just like that.

The calm waves—both figurative and literal—washed over her. The orgasm wasn't like anything she'd experienced before. It wasn't mind-blowing but it was sweet, perfect, and everything she hadn't realized she'd been missing. Something told her he'd been holding back for her, giving her exactly what she needed at that moment. If he'd pushed her too far, too fast and made her feel too out of control she wouldn't have been able to handle it. But this…she wanted more of him and what he could give her. She'd had no idea things could be like that between two people.

Such pleasure at the hands of a man was an odd, but liberating experience. Somehow she knew this was just the beginning. If he could do that with just his mouth and a bare rub of his finger, then what would he do when they finally got to the part where they were both actually naked?

As she came down from her high, he held her steady. Thankfully, his breathing was just as labored as hers. She should feel some semblance of modesty, but for the life of her, she didn't care that she was still partially exposed. She was comfortable with her body, but being naked around men was unusual. And in the daylight? That was a new experience altogether.

"Wow." The word didn't come close to describing how she felt, but it was all she could manage.

"Wow is right." His face broke into a grin. A satisfied, pure male grin.

"I hope that's only a preview of what's to come." The words were out before she could censor herself. *Holy shit, where had that come from?*

His eyes widened slightly, but he sighed in relief.

"What?"

"I was hoping you'd say something like that." His grip tightened on her hips and his eyes darkened.

She pulled up her bathing suit straps but stayed in his lap, comfortable enough to stay there all afternoon. "As opposed to what?"

He shrugged, but kept his arms around. "I thought you might say something about this being a mistake."

She chuckled, enjoying the way he held her. His embrace was almost protective, and though it surprised her, she didn't want to move. "This probably *is* a mistake, but it's one I'd make again."

"Good." After what felt like an eternity, he finally disentangled himself and helped her to her feet.

She wasn't quite sure what to say. It wasn't that she was embarrassed, but she did feel a little awkward. Where would they go from here? They certainly couldn't go back in time and change things. And she didn't want to. Still, with everything going on, she wasn't sure if she could handle anything else.

"Are you hungry?" he asked as they picked up their towels and clothes.

"A little," she admitted. "But, what about…what about you?" She didn't have the guts to voice what she meant explicitly, but he seemed to understand.

"We'll worry about that later. I'm in no rush," he murmured before planting a kiss on her forehead. He casually wrapped his arm around her shoulders as they walked back to the house.

Her experience was limited, but as far as men went, they normally couldn't wait to get to the next part. And he wanted to wait? She'd thought for sure she had his type pegged.

For once, Hope didn't mind being wrong.

* * * * *

Mac tossed his suitcase onto one of the double beds in his hotel room. Now that he was checked into a hotel in Miami, he had to make the call he'd been dreading. Before he told Hope his suspicions, he was going to meet the Santiago family face to face. Instead of using his cell phone he used the hotel phone. The only number that would come up on caller ID would be the main line. And he wanted them to know he was in town.

Someone picked up on the second ring. "Santiago residence."

His throat clenched, and he wiped a sweaty palm on his jeans. What the hell? He'd been in tougher situations than this.

"Hello?" The woman on the other line sounded annoyed.

He cleared his throat. "Hi, is Mrs. Santiago in?"

"May I ask who is calling?"

She had no idea who he was, so he doubted the woman would even relay the message, but he didn't have a choice in giving his name. "My name is Mac Jennings."

The response was automatic. "I'm sorry Mr. Jennings, she's unavailable—" Muffled, indistinct voices traveled through the line.

Seconds later, another woman was on the phone. "This is Sonja Santiago. How can I help you?" Her voice was soft, almost reserved, but he didn't miss her anxiety.

He swallowed hard. This was more difficult than he'd imagined. "Hi, my name is Mac Jennings. You hired my daughter for the month...I don't even know where to start."

"I think I have an idea why you're calling. Would you like to do this in person?"

His heart pounded against his ribcage at hurricane speeds. The fact that she wasn't surprised by his call spoke volumes. "Name the place."

"I'll send a car to pick you up. You're staying at the Hyatt, correct?"

"Yes. When would you like to meet?" He clutched the phone tighter.

"Can you be ready in twenty minutes?"

"I'll be down in the lobby in ten."

"Perfect." She disconnected before he could ask how he'd know who to look for.

A little over twenty minutes later, he sat in the back of a Lincoln Town car, on his way to the Santiagos' house. Never before in his life had he felt so lost. Mac took life in stride. He always had. When he'd lost his wife and daughter, his ability to compartmentalize things had saved his sanity. Now things were different. Hope had saved his life more than he'd ever admitted. She was more than just a girl he'd helped raise, she was his family. Closer to him than any blood relatives he had left.

He didn't know anything about this other family other than what he'd read in a few files, but if they were Hope's blood relations, she had a right to know. He just prayed she still wanted him in her life if they turned out to be who he thought they were.

Palm trees, people, and colorful buildings flew by at normal speeds, but Mac felt as if his insides were actually shaking. After ten minutes in the car, the driver pulled into a private, gated community, right on the bay. Of course they pulled into the driveway of the biggest house in the secluded neighborhood. When the car pulled to a stop in front of a Tuscan-style villa, he got out before the driver could come around and open his door.

Almost immediately, the intricately carved wooden front door opened and a woman with a startling resemblance to Hope stepped out. Right behind her were two men with holstered guns. He instantly went on alert. Maybe this wasn't the friendly visit he'd expected.

She made the first move and walked the few feet

toward him. She held out a delicate hand. "Hi, I'm Sonja. Welcome to my home."

He nodded and took her hand in his own. "Mac. Pleased to meet you."

"Would you like to speak out on the lanai? It's much more comfortable." Her words sounded sincere, but stress lines etched deep into her fair face.

The two men disappeared back inside, but he knew they weren't far away. He guessed they'd only wanted to make their presence known.

As they walked through the foyer, he paused at a display of pictures and picked one up. "Shit." The word was out before he could think. He had the pictures from Howard, but looking at the massive display of photographs of the Santiagos' daughter Maria, the resemblance was unmistakable. And terrifying.

Sonja looked at him with eyebrows raised, but didn't say anything. Her pale blue eyes were so much like Hope's his heart twisted.

He put the picture back on the table and followed her down a long hallway lined with other, similar photos. They exited out a back door and settled across from each other at a rectangular glass patio table.

For a moment they stared at each other, and he wasn't sure if he should start talking first.

She beat him to it and her question surprised him. "What is she like?"

"She's...she's like sunshine." It sounded cheesy, but it was the only word he could think to describe Hope. She'd been a handful that first year. So angry at everyone, but she'd learned to defend herself and had developed a steel backbone. Sometimes he worried he'd been too tough on her, but as she'd seen, the world was a shitty place and he'd wanted her to be able to take care of herself.

There was another moment of extended silence. An

older gentleman delivering a tray of iced tea and lemonade interrupted them, but a few minutes later they were alone again.

"What…how…" She raked a shaky hand through her long hair and expelled a sigh. "I'm sorry, I don't know where to start."

"You're not alone." He took one of the glasses to keep his hands busy.

"Where did you adopt her? On the black market?" Her quiet question sliced through the air with the subtlety of a grenade.

"What? I think you have the wrong idea. I *found* Hope when she was fifteen. She had nowhere to go." He left it at that for the moment.

Waves of almost visible relief poured off the other woman. "I had to ask. Luke ran your information and it didn't seem likely, but we haven't been able to find out much about you. And Hope Jennings didn't exist until twelve years ago. Is she…was she a runaway?"

"Not exactly." He risked everything he'd struggled to hide for over a decade, but it was a choice he had to make. Mac decided not to edge around the truth. "Twelve years ago I found a fifteen year old girl floating just off the coast."

"Floating?" Sonja's hand flew to her neck, and her forehead furrowed in confusion.

He nodded and forced himself to continue. If this was Hope's mother, nothing about this was going to be easy. "She'd been shot twice and was barely alive." His words dropped like deadly bombs, and all he could do was wait for the reaction.

A mix between a sob and a shriek exploded from the other woman. A man with a gun stormed out one of the French doors, but she shooed him away without glancing in his direction. She clutched the side of her chair, her pale eyes boring into him. "I don't understand."

Mac inwardly cursed. Maybe he should have left that part out. It had happened so long ago and he sometimes lacked the sensitive gene. "Do you want to get a real drink?"

She abruptly stood, though her entire body shook. "Yes, this calls for vodka."

Considering how much more he had to tell her, she was definitely going to need it.

Hell, he was too.

He watched as she walked over to the mini bar on the other side of the lanai. Her hands were unsteady as she added cubes of ice to two glasses. Normally he'd offer to help a woman, but he guessed she needed to gain some control.

She glanced over at him as she pulled out a bottle of vodka. "Is tonic as a mixer okay?"

"Yes." At this point, he didn't care what he drank, as long as it was wet.

Moments later, she handed him a glass and sat back down across from him.

He took a swig, then placed the drink on the table. "Some of the things I have to say will be unpleasant. Do you want—"

"I want to know *everything* about her."

Mac mentally steeled himself to deal with a crying woman. No parent should have to hear what she was about to. "According to Hope, she'd been in the foster system since she was seven. When she was fifteen, one of her foster father's basically sold her to cover some debts. He reported her as a runaway."

"Sold? I don't understand."

Fuck. How could he tell her this? He cleared his throat. "She was sold into…sexual slavery."

Despite the woman's gasp, he continued. If he didn't tell her now, he didn't think he'd ever get it out. "There is no good way to say this. The first man she was…sold

90

to, had a yacht. That's all she knows about him. He raped her, but she fought back and he shot her in the process. She fell overboard and was no doubt assumed dead. I found her and adopted her."

"Why didn't you call the police?"

"I had to make a quick decision that night. I wasn't going to put her back into the system that had already failed her." The truth was, Hope had begged him not to call the police. If Mac could go back, he didn't know that he'd do things any differently. She'd been an abused, terrorized kid and he'd have sold his soul to help her that night.

"How did you manage to adopt her and change her identity?" Sonja set her drink down and laced her fingers tightly in her lap.

This was the tricky part. Figuring out how much to admit to this virtual stranger. "To make a long story short, I called in some favors." A hell of a lot of them.

"Those are some pretty big favors."

He shrugged, unwilling to divulge any more at the moment.

"Fair enough," she murmured. After a long beat, she spoke again. "If you're willing, I'd like you to stay and have dinner with me. I understand if you can't answer them all, but I have so many questions."

"Okay." He sighed and took another sip of his drink. If this was Hope's family, she deserved to meet them. Years before he'd found Hope he'd lost a wife and daughter. The grief had nearly killed him. He knew his thoughts were selfish, but he couldn't help and wonder what would happen if she met the Santiagos' and didn't need him anymore.

Mac didn't know if he'd survive losing Hope.

Chapter 8

Luke started a pot of coffee, hoping the aroma or obnoxious noise he was making banging around coffee cups would wake Hope. It was only eight, but he'd been awake for two hours and his mind was going into overdrive. He still had a hard time believing what had happened between them yesterday. Even more startling, how normal things had been between them the rest of the day. The intensity with which he wanted to see her rattled him to his core.

Normally he liked his space in the mornings, even when he was seeing someone. Okay, especially when he was dating someone. This morning was different.

Today would be the real test. Now that she'd had time to think about it, he wondered if she might be regretting their kiss and…after. He still couldn't believe how quickly she'd responded to his caresses. She'd seemed to think he'd wanted more after that kiss—which he had—but not yet. The timing wasn't right. Kissing and stroking her like that had short-circuited his brain. He needed to get a handle on that before moving any further.

If he fucked things up he'd never forgive himself.

As he pulled down two mugs from one of the cabinets, he sensed her enter the room.

"Hey." She hung back in the doorway, shifting from one foot to the other, her voice as tentative as her body language. Her hands clasped tightly in front of her, she looked as if she was ready to bolt back to her room.

"Hey yourself. Want some?" He lifted his mug.

She nodded and her shoulders slightly relaxed.

He poured her a mug and when he handed it to her, he leaned in and dropped a kiss on her lips somewhere between chaste and sensual. Someone had to break the ice and he needed to taste her like he needed his next breath. "Minty," he murmured against her mouth

A real smile tugged at her lips and she leaned into him. "Have you eaten breakfast, yet?"

"No. Are you hungry?"

She shook her head and took a sip of her coffee. "How late did you stay up researching Richard Taylor?" Her voice was wary.

"Until about midnight."

"Did you find out anything interesting?" She leaned against the counter, a few feet from him, and the yoga style pants she wore shifted a couple inches lower, revealing more of her taut stomach.

He forced himself to think about her question and not what was underneath her clothes. And definitely not what he wanted to do to her once he got them off her. "Nothing interesting." That wasn't entirely true. His partner had called again upon discovering Richard Taylor had nearly tripled his fortune in the past decade, and that in addition to being involved in biotechnology, he was also associated with a few social deviants. Who the man associated with might mean nothing, but somehow Luke doubted it.

He paused as he weighed his options. "Did you call anyone yesterday?"

She answered without pause. "I called Mac."

"I figured. What did he say?" He understood why

she'd called him, he just didn't like it. He'd called his partner too, but Luke didn't know anything about her father and he didn't like dealing with unknown variables.

The clock was ticking and after tomorrow they'd be heading to Miami—unless something new came up—and he still had no clue how to tell her she looked exactly like his missing childhood friend.

"Just to stay put and that he'd figure something out." She took another sip of her coffee and averted her gaze.

Okay. She was lying. He was finding it easier and easier to read her expressions.

"He sure took everything in stride." He couldn't hide his sarcasm.

Instantly she bristled at his words and her voice had an unmistakable edge. "What's that supposed to mean?"

He shrugged. "I expected more of a reaction from a father for his daughter in danger." He knew he was playing with fire trying to figure out more about her past. The second the words were out of his mouth, he knew he'd made a mistake.

A big one.

"Don't you talk about my relationship with him. *Ever.*" She placed the coffee cup in the sink, threw him a disparaging look, and disappeared into her room. She didn't slam the door, though he'd anticipated it.

He'd have felt better if she'd yelled at him or shown some sort of outward response. Quiet anger wasn't something he was equipped to deal with. Maria Santiago, her look-alike, acted like a spoiled child most of the time. She wasn't a brat, she'd just been incredibly sheltered.

Minutes later, he still stood in the middle of the kitchen trying to figure out an apology when Hope walked out wearing a skimpy bikini and carrying a towel and a book. Without a word or even a glance in his direction, she exited out the back door. For a long moment all he could focus on was the soft sway of her barely covered ass. The bright red bikini bottom bared the bottom of her cheeks and made his cock flare to life. *Damn.* He could easily imagine running his palms over that smooth skin.

He inwardly cursed his own stupidity. Instead of gaining her confidence, he'd alienated her and now it looked as if she was teasing him. He watched through the window as she stretched out on one of the lounge chairs and began rubbing sunscreen on her lean legs. If she'd worn the revealing bathing suit to affect him, it had worked. She might as well have been naked. The two bright red triangle strips barely covered her nipples.

He rubbed a hand over his face and turned away from the window. *Think.* They would be leaving soon and he still hadn't made progress in discovering who she was. If he wasted time staring at her practically naked body he'd only torture himself.

While she was preoccupied, he decided to take advantage. He might regret it later, but it also might clear up the question of who Hope really was. This might be his only chance. He grabbed two plastic sandwich-size bags from one of the kitchen drawers, then after another glance outside, he rushed to her bathroom. After replacing her toothbrush with an exact spare from the cabinet, he pulled a few strands of hair from her hairbrush, but not enough that she would notice anything. Then he put both items in separate baggies.

Heart pounding, he retrieved his wallet and keys before scrawling a note that he'd be gone for an hour. He considered asking if she needed anything from town, but he didn't want to risk that she'd want to come with him. For a few long moments he sat in the vehicle and stared down at what he'd taken. What he was doing was wrong. He knew that on every level.

But Sonja needed to know for her own sanity. How could he let her down after all these years? After he'd played a part in her daughter's disappearance?

Shaking off the guilt—or at least burying it for the moment—he started the engine and steered out of the driveway. The consequences might kill him, but he had to do this. He owed it to the Santiagos.

* * * * *

After reading the same page thirteen times, Hope threw her book down and flipped onto her stomach. Luke certainly had some nerve. They might have shared something yesterday, but he had no right to talk about her father. Maybe she'd overreacted, but his condescending attitude rankled her. She couldn't believe she'd been contemplating sleeping with him.

Okay, that wasn't true. She was still thinking about it, but only as a test. She hadn't ever had truly enjoyable sex. It had been tolerable, if a little awkward, and the single reason she'd even attempted it was because her therapist had thought it would be a good idea.

Part of her was glad she knew that she was capable of having sex, but another part of her wondered what she'd been missing. Her friends and dive buddies always talked about it. Hell, everyone always seemed to be talking about it, so she knew it had to be better than what she'd experienced.

Luke was the perfect candidate to prove her right. After this job was done she wouldn't have to see him again. They could get hot and heavy and she could completely indulge herself with him with no strings attached. The thought sounded almost cold to her, but she couldn't help herself. She wanted to experience— and enjoy—what almost everyone on the planet did.

Everything that had happened in the past few days

had jolted her out of her sense of security. She knew firsthand the world was full of monsters, but living in The Keys, she'd almost convinced herself that she was now safe from the world.

Whatever the future held, she decided she wasn't going to die never having experienced great—no, mind blowing—sex. Luke had already given her a preview of what he could do, so she knew she wouldn't be disappointed. With that thought, she closed her eyes and let the sound of the ocean lull her to sleep.

Hope wasn't sure how much time passed, but woke up to the feel of a warm, strong hand gently shaking her shoulder. Considering what she and Luke had just run from maybe she should have been afraid but before she even turned over, she knew it was Luke.

That callused hand on her shoulder was just so damn gentle.

She rolled over onto her back to find him staring down at her. Perched on the side of her lounge chair, his expression was dark and almost predatory. Something in that charcoal gaze of his made every primal part of her tingle in awareness. Sudden heat flooded between her legs. Trying to be discrete she clenched her legs together.

"What's wrong?" She raised her hand to block out the sun streaming through the palm tree leaves and to better gauge his expression.

His jaw clenched and he shook his head. She guessed that meant nothing was wrong.

But his silence worried her. "Are you okay?" She propped herself up on one elbow.

He still didn't answer.

A burst of panic popped inside her. She sat straight up, ready to run if he gave the word. Her heart pounded an erratic tattoo against her chest. "Have we been—"

Whatever she'd been about to say was silenced when

his mouth slanted over hers. If his kisses had been soft and gentle before, they weren't now. Now, his lips were hard and demanding. Sensual and searching with each stroke. Instinctively, her hands flew to his chest. Instead of pushing him away, her fingers dug in, needing to feel him in a way she didn't understand. Had never experienced before. All that muscle under her touch made her entire body hum with anticipation.

When he pulled away she started to protest, but he simply dipped his head to her jaw and began feathering kisses along her skin. "Did you wear this sexy suit to drive me insane?" he murmured against her ear as he nipped the sensitive lobe.

She swallowed and tried to comprehend his words. How could she think right now? And what had brought on the sudden onslaught of his attention? It seemed all he had to do was touch her and she was on fire.

"Did you?" he growled again.

How was the man even talking? "Yes," she managed to gasp out as he raked his teeth over her pulse point. The thought that she was supposed to be angry with him briefly entered her thoughts, but she quickly dismissed it. Being angry was boring and what they were doing was so much more fun.

"I thought so." He kissed her deeply again before wrenching away. "Shit," he muttered, then stood and turned his back to her. His neck muscles were corded so tightly, he looked ready to snap.

"Luke?"

He sat back down. His breathing was erratic, but he eventually spoke. "This probably isn't the best idea. Until we figure out what's going on, maybe we should—"

She placed a finger on his mouth. If that's all he was worried about, then he could forget it. She'd tell him later that she knew who was after her, but not now. She didn't want to ruin the moment. Now, she simply wanted to be selfish for once. "I want you. Now."

His gaze went so dark, so *hungry*, it made her shiver. Without a word, he took her hand, and they walked inside. Well, she more or less floated. Once they reached his bedroom, she couldn't remember actually moving through the house. Her head was fuzzy, as if she were dreaming. Hope knew what was going to happen, and feelings of giddy anticipation and fear waged war inside her body. Maybe this was how she was supposed to feel.

They stood at the foot of the bed, silent, staring at each other. The lust in his eyes was obvious and potent and it scared the hell out of her. She could handle the sweet and gentle Luke, but she didn't know if she could handle this side of him.

"Are you sure this is what you want?" His voice had dropped a few octaves. It was low, sensual, and drugging to her senses.

She nodded before she found her voice. "Yes."

Slowly, methodically, he reached around and pulled the flimsy ties loose from around her neck and back. The scrap of material silently fell to the floor and she shivered. Whether from the cool draft or his intense gaze, she didn't know. Her nipples peaked almost painfully she was so aroused. And the heat between her legs grew more with each second that passed.

She looped her arms around his neck as he kissed her again. At the same time, he wrapped his arms around her waist and started to lay her onto the bed. Automatically, she hooked both legs around him, pulling him with her onto the bed. She groaned at the feel of his erection rubbing against her. Arching her back, she savored the feel of her breasts rubbing against his shirt—and wished he was naked. It was hard not to feel like an animal in heat as she rubbed against him, but it was also hard to care. The man made her absolutely crazy. She wanted him to completely cover her with his body. To surround and devour her. She needed him so bad her entire body ached for it.

Suddenly he stilled. His entire body covered hers, but he was immobile. Her breath hitched, wondering what was wrong. He couldn't stop now. She'd die of frustration. And embarrassment. Maybe he'd changed his mind about her.

Their faces were now inches apart and she could feel hers start to heat up. If he had changed his mind she would will the floor to open up and swallow her whole.

"You're perfect," he said the words solemnly, reverently, and her heart twisted.

He'd said the same thing the day before, and she hadn't known how to respond then either. Her scars were hideous, both the outward and internal ones, and he didn't care. How could she not melt when he touched her? When he looked at her as if she were the most precious thing in the world.

Unable to find words, she tugged his shirt over his head and he pushed off his cargo shorts in a few quick moves. The need to feel his naked body against hers was a living breathing thing inside her. Before she had a chance to completely enjoy his naked body, he leaned over and pulled a condom from the nightstand. Never before had she found the act interesting, but she couldn't tear her eyes away from his hands. With strong, lean fingers he rolled the condom over his cock. At the sight, her lower abdomen clenched almost painfully tight. The only thing left between them now was her bathing suit bottom.

Her insides felt as if they were actually trembling and she was thankful she was lying down. If she'd been standing, she wasn't sure she could have trusted her knees to hold her up. She was about to have sex with the hottest man she'd ever met, and her senses were going into overload.

He settled in between her legs, his cock brushing the covered opening of her wet sheath. All it would take was a few moves and she'd be completely bared for him. Since he was hardly moving, she propped up on her elbows, pushing her breasts up farther and feeling more exposed than ever. But, she didn't care. "What are you waiting for?"

The corners of his mouth curled up slightly. Surprisingly, his hands shook as he untied the side bows of her bathing suit bottom. That meant he was just as anxious as her.

Thank goodness.

She inhaled his pure male scent as he trailed kisses along her neck and jaw. The licking and teasing of his tongue stoked her desire even hotter. Instead of penetrating, he rubbed against her open folds. The feel of all that hardness lightly stroking her most intimate area only made her inner walls clench with unfilled need.

She knew he was trying to give her more foreplay, but she didn't want to wait. Not this time. Her body knew what it wanted. Before she could question herself, she adjusted her hips and impaled herself on him. She gasped as she adjusted to his size.

"Oh god," he murmured against her ear as he found his rhythm.

My sentiments exactly, she thought. Sleeping with him might be the biggest mistake of her life. Or the most amazing experience of her life. Hell, it might be a bit of both.

Their bodies meshed together in a frenetic dance. She'd always wanted sex soft and slow, but this time she needed it hard and fast. Luke wasn't going to hurt her. Her head knew it and now so did her body.

She was finally free to enjoy herself. And her body screamed for release.

He somehow understood every nuance of her body. With expert hands, he gently tweaked and pulled her nipples, sending erotic pulses straight to her core. At the same time, his mouth never left hers. As if he understood her need for a certain kind of closeness now.

The faster his thrusts, the closer she came to release. When he reached between their bodies and brushed his thumb over her clit, it was the final stimulation she needed. Her orgasm hit hard and fast. In an almost violent release, her entire body shook and pulsed with flowing pleasure. She tightened her legs around him and just as quickly as she'd come, so did he.

His climax was wild and raw and pure male. He shouted her name as he came, the sound shocking her. After he rode through his orgasm, he gently pulled out of her and rolled onto his back, but kept one hand touching her side, as if he needed that connection.

Hope kicked the tangle of sheets away as she laid there. In more ways than one, she was too hot to breathe or move. A light sheen of sweat had formed across her forehead but she was too lethargic to wipe it away. She just wanted to bask in the afterglow of her bliss.

After a few minutes had passed, Luke propped up on one elbow and grinned down at her, the smile totally masculine.

"What?" She wasn't sure if she liked that look on his face.

"I hope you're not tired because that was round one." He bent down and nipped her earlobe.

"I like the sound of that," she murmured.

As he moved back on top of her, delivering kisses along her jaw and neck, she wrapped her arms around him. She traced her fingers down his back until she gripped his backside. "Tell me about the tattoo on your butt."

He stopped mid-kiss and looked up to meet her gaze

and an almost comical expression crossed his face. Like a kid caught stealing candy from his mother's purse. "You saw that?"

She tried to suppress a laugh as he cringed. "Kinda hard to miss it."

He dropped his head onto her chest and groaned. "I got it when I was in the Marines."

She bit her bottom lip. "Why the Road Runner?"

He lifted his head, his expression almost mournful. "Because I was young and stupid. One drunk night, five of us decided to get inked. I'm just glad I didn't end up with Tweety Bird."

She dug her hands into his flesh and allowed herself to laugh. "Because that would have been so much worse?"

"Hey now." He leaned down and nipped her bottom lip playfully.

Instinctively she wrapped her legs around him, pulling him closer. There was still a lot she didn't know about Luke, but the more she learned, the more she realized she could actually fall for him. Something that scared the hell out of her.

* * * * *

Luke lay staring at the ceiling. Still asleep, Hope curled up against the length of his body. She hadn't moved much in the past thirty minutes he'd been awake. Neither had he, but only because he didn't want to wake her. They hadn't left the bed the day before except to eat and that had only been at her insistence. He could have stayed there all day and been satisfied. A few hours before dawn she'd finally collapsed, but he couldn't seem to find any peace in sleep. His thoughts were too occupied with Hope. Way too occupied.

He'd always enjoyed sex as much as the next guy,

but if a woman wasn't available, his fist was fine. Now, he couldn't imagine fucking—making love—to anyone but Hope. He shook his head. Since when did he think of it as making love anyway?

It was the third day they'd been in hiding and he wanted to call his partner, but figured letting Hope sleep in couldn't hurt. He'd worn her out and she deserved her rest.

When she threw a silky leg over his waist, he groaned. Maybe he wouldn't let her sleep. He traced a finger up and down her spine, savoring the satiny feel of her back. After a few minutes of his stroking, she opened her eyes and looked up at him, a tiny smile tugging at her lips.

"How long have you been awake?" she murmured as she shifted onto her back.

He propped up on one elbow and stretched out next to her, enjoying the view of her perfect breasts and tanned body. "Not long."

She smiled, now more awake, and pulled him so that he was fully on top of her. He wouldn't have thought it possible she'd want more, but the woman was insatiable. His cock lengthened against her slick folds, but he didn't penetrate her.

"Tell me about this." He traced a finger over the webbed scar on her shoulder.

Immediately, she shut down. Before she even moved, it was as if she was physically pulling away from him. Then she did just that. Shifting out of his embrace, she sat up and scooted to the edge of the bed. When she reached for one of his shirts he grabbed her around her waist and pulled her back against him. Her body was curved into his chest, her smooth back against his much rougher body. She didn't try to fight him, but her entire body was pulled tight. After what they'd shared last night he couldn't let her put distance between them.

"Why can't I ask questions?" he murmured against her ear.

A light shudder rolled through her, but her back was still ramrod straight. So he waited until finally she slumped against him. "You can ask all the questions you want, I just might not answer them," she said softly.

"So you'll share your body with me, but you won't answer a simple question?" His jaw clenched but he tried to keep the heat out of his voice.

She shook her head, and her dark hair tickled his face. "I'd rather not answer than lie to you."

Sighing, he moved back so they could face each other. How could he argue with that? When she turned around, he dropped a kiss on her forehead. "I guess I can live with that." *For now anyway.*

"Good." Relief instantly flooded her expression. Without pause, she leaned forward and brushed her lips over his.

His cock, which hadn't gone down any, felt as if it hardened even more. Her delicate fingers clutched on to his shoulders as she straddled him. As her tongue danced against his in an erotic frenzy, he knew he'd let practically anything go if she kissed him like this. How sad was that?

When the buzz of his phone interrupted them, she smiled against his lips and fell back against the pillow with a groan. "You better answer that."

He wanted to argue, but she was right. The number wasn't familiar, but the area code was from the Virginia/DC area so he flipped the cell open. "Yeah?" He didn't answer with his name intentionally.

"You're free to return to Miami now," an unfamiliar voice said.

"What?"

"Turn on the news."

The line disconnected before he could ask anything.

"Who was that?" He was disappointed to find Hope had put on a long T-shirt.

"I don't know." Luke grabbed the remote and turned on the television. After flipping through a few local channels, he found the world news.

"What are you doing?" Hope scooted up to the edge of the bed and sat next to him, her thigh pressing against his.

"I'm not sure yet…" He turned up the volume when a video of Richard Taylor flashed on screen.

Two men in suits were putting a handcuffed Taylor into a dark car. Photographers snapped pictures and journalists shouted out questions, but he kept his head down and never responded. A byline ran across the bottom of the screen. *Biotech mogul arrested on suspicion of espionage, tax fraud, and human trafficking.*

"Holy crap," Hope muttered.

"My thoughts, exactly." He rubbed a hand over his face. This was a good thing. In his head he knew that. They needed to get back to civilization, but now he'd have to tell Hope the truth about his suspicions.

For several minutes, neither spoke as they watched the screen in fascination.

"What do you think he's going to do when he finds out I'm still alive?" she asked suddenly.

"Believe me, you're the least of his worries. Espionage is a capital offense."

Another byline ran across the screen stating that his son had disappeared, but was also wanted on suspicion of human trafficking. Next to him, Hope shivered but didn't comment.

He reached out to pull her close when his phone buzzed again.

"Have you seen the news?" His partner asked before he could say hello.

"Sure did."

"I assume you're coming back to Miami now?"

"I need to work some things out, but yeah. I'll be in touch. Oh, one more thing. Have you talked to Maria lately?"

"Yeah, why?"

"She's called me a few times, but I obviously haven't called back. You haven't said anything to her about what's going on, have you?"

"No. Why would I?" His partner's voice was suddenly heated.

"Uh, it was just a question."

He glanced at Hope, who wasn't paying any attention to him as she still stared at the television.

"Sorry man, I know. I'm just tense," Kyle said.

"What's going on?"

Kyle sighed. "Nothing I can't handle. There have been some strange things going on at the main plant in Costa Rica. Eduardo's been checking in and keeping me updated, but I can't shake the feeling that something's off. I'm thinking this might be an inside job."

Eduardo was one of the new guys they'd hired and so far he was more than capable. Still, Kyle should have told him they were having problems. Lately Kyle had seemed distracted and Luke couldn't figure out what was going on with his partner.

"Why didn't you mention anything?"

"You've got a lot on your plate right now and I didn't want to bother you with something as trivial as missing shipments. If it gets worse, I'll let you know."

"All right. We'll be in town tonight. If I need anything I'll call you."

As soon as they disconnected, Hope glanced over. "Who was that and where will we be tonight?"

He shook his head and chuckled. She'd obviously been paying more attention than he'd thought. "That was my partner and if we can get a flight out, we'll be in

Miami tonight."

She pursed her lips into a thin line. "We will?"

"Even with Taylor in jail, I don't think it's smart for you to go home. Come to Miami for a few days...please. I'm in the security business and I guarantee I can protect you better than anyone." He couldn't force her to come with him and he knew Sonja didn't care about the job anyway. Hope had been hired because of her face.

"Okay." She shook her head and took a few steps toward the doorway. "I'll go pack, then."

She turned on her heel and even though he wanted to stop her and kiss her until neither one of them could think straight, he knew he couldn't. He had too many phone calls to make and too much to do.

* * * * *

Hope dialed Mac for the tenth time, then threw her phone in her purse. It kept going straight to voicemail and that wasn't like him. Because of her crazy schedule, he normally had his phone attached to his hip. She prayed he hadn't done anything stupid. Mac kept his promises, but she knew how he could get when he was angry enough. Pushing aside her worry, she scanned the room one more time before hauling her bag out to the kitchen. Wrapping her arms around her body, she stared out the window, prepping herself for their trip.

True to his word, Luke had chartered a private plane for them straight to Miami. She was a little nervous about meeting Sonja Santiago since most of her gear had been left behind in Cuba. Luke assured her that he'd had it taken care of and everything had been shipped directly to the Santiagos' home, but what if it hadn't been packaged right? If word got out that she'd screwed up a big job it could ruin her reputation and repeat business. And what if...?

She stopped herself. There wasn't anything she could do about it now.

"You ready?" Luke's voice cut into her thoughts.

She turned around from staring out the window to meet his dark gaze. "Yes." As ready as she'd ever be.

He grabbed her bags, so she followed him in silence. He didn't seem to want to talk and that was fine with her.

All day Luke had been on the phone and she hadn't been able to contact the one person she needed. On top of that, she was annoyed with herself. Even though she'd sworn she only wanted to have a physical relationship with him, she couldn't deny her growing feelings.

And he hadn't so much as hinted at what he thought or wanted.

Men.

Chapter 9

Patrick Taylor paced back and forth in the dingy motel room he was staying in right outside of Coconut Grove. It smelled of vomit and old Chinese food, but he had no choice other than to stay there. He couldn't use his credit cards anywhere, and if he attempted to touch his known bank accounts, the FBI would find him. Sure, he had a lot of extra cash, but he was pretty sure the Feds were watching for him. No one in their right mind would expect him to stay in a dump like this. Even if he could use his cards he wouldn't try to stay anywhere above a two-star rating. This place probably ranked half a star.

His father was in jail, the FBI was looking for him, and he was ninety-nine percent sure that bitch was still alive. Considering the man who was supposed to kill her was an undercover FBI agent, he'd bet his trust fund she was still breathing.

The phone in the room rang twice, then stopped. Ten seconds later it rang again, so he picked it up immediately. "Yeah?"

"I think I've got what you want," the familiar, scratchy voice said.

"Good." Patrick savored the small moment of relief he experienced because he knew it wouldn't last.

"It's gonna cost you."

What else was new? "My lawyer has already wired half your fee. You'll get the rest when I get what I want."

There was a long pause. This was normally how they worked, but he wasn't in a position to bargain. If the other man demanded full payment now, he'd have to give it to him.

"Fine. The man she was with chartered a plane out of the Bahamas today. They should be in Miami soon and I know where he lives."

The address he rattled off was an exclusive condo community right on South Beach. Before Patrick could voice his concern, the other man continued.

"Don't bother trying to get to her there. This guy is in the protection business and even though I couldn't find out much about him, his building has some of the best security in the industry."

"I'm not stupid." Patrick rolled his eyes. Getting her alone was the only thing he'd consider.

The other man snorted, but Patrick couldn't afford to show his annoyance.

"I'll be in contact in a few days," Patrick said.

"Don't forget, in one week your window of opportunity closes."

"I haven't forgot."

The line went dead and Patrick cursed as he poured another scotch. He hadn't forgotten anything. He had to get out of the country and his way out was only available for a week. Hell, he would leave right now if it wasn't for *her*. Everything else he was dealing with paled in comparison to having a live witness. She was the only real threat in his life. One he thought had disappeared years ago.

He put on a dark ball cap, grabbed another drink for the road and headed out. As a precaution, he flipped the door sign to read do not disturb. He didn't have anything worth stealing except his computer, and he couldn't risk that falling into the wrong hands.

* * * * *

"Are you sure you don't want me to stay at a hotel?" Hope asked for the second time since they'd landed in Miami.

"No. I'm not letting you out of my sight, so please drop it," Luke said as he steered his truck into the secure parking garage of his private building.

She wrapped her arms around herself. "I know that. I was just thinking we could both stay at a hotel. I don't want to put you out or be an inconvenience."

"It's not a problem." He put the car in park and jumped out. Ever since she'd found out it was safe to return to the States, she'd been quiet. Unusually so. He didn't know how to pull her back out of her shell. He'd expected that once they slept together she'd be more at ease around him, but if anything she'd pulled further away from him.

She walked around to the back of his truck and tugged out one of the smaller bags. Under her breath, she mumbled something about him being stubborn.

He'd been called worse.

He shook his head, but didn't comment as they walked toward the elevators. The only sound in the garage was the snapping of her flip-flops against the cement. Once they reached the elevators, he typed in the fifteen digit code.

"No wonder you wanted to stay here," Hope said as they stepped inside.

He adjusted one of the bags over his shoulder. "Are you hungry?" Maybe that would get her talking.

Her eyes lit up and she half-smiled. "Starving."

"How about I order Chinese? Unless you'd like

something different." The elevator halted at the top floor. He got out first as a precaution. Since he owned the entire floor, he hadn't expected to see anyone, but he relaxed slightly at the empty corridor.

"Chinese or pizza works for me." She trailed behind him. "Wait a minute, is this whole floor just you?" Her eyes widened.

The elevator opened into a big foyer-type area and there was only one door so it was a good guess he owned everything. He cleared his throat, suddenly embarrassed, but he didn't know why it should bother her. "Yeah."

"Oh." The way she said it tore at his insides.

She shifted from foot to foot as he opened the door and he wished he could figure out what was going on in that pretty head of hers. The expression on her face told him she'd rather be anywhere but there. Which really sucked since he didn't want to be anywhere but with her.

He held open the door for her and she eyed him warily as she passed by.

"Where should I put my stuff?"

"Follow me." He led her to the guest room closest to his.

His condo was sparse and he'd never cared before. Now he wished he'd done something to make it look like more than a cold hotel. The guest room with its adjoining bathroom had a queen-size bed, a nightstand with a lamp and not much else. The floor was tile, and when he saw her expression, he realized just how sterile the room actually was.

She cleared her throat and looked pointedly at the bag he still held.

"Oh, right. Here." He dropped the bag at the end of the bed. The thud echoed loudly against the tile. "I'll order food and meet you out in the living room in a while."

"Thanks." She nodded and clutched her purse against

her stomach.

Sighing, he closed the door behind him and leaned against it. What had happened to distance her so much in the past day? It seemed like once they'd left the Caribbean she put that damn wall back up again. It shredded his insides. If she thought she could erect barriers between them after the connection they'd made she was out of her damn mind.

* * * * *

Hope let the shower jets massage her shoulders. Somehow she had to ease her tension. That monster was still missing and even though his father was in jail, she wasn't so sure she was safe.

Luke had said he'd protect her, but he didn't know what she was running from, and she certainly wasn't offering up that information. Not yet, anyway. She needed to get Mac's opinion on things first. If she was honest with herself, what she really needed was to wrap her head around her growing feelings for Luke. On a certain level she knew she could trust him, but saying the words aloud, admitting what she'd been through was something she'd rather ignore and put off for as long as she could. Part of her wanted to return home tonight. She and Mac could take care of themselves. Still, she felt she should at least meet the woman who had hired her. She wasn't worried about getting out of the contract. After everything that had happened, she doubted they cared about her finishing the job. Luke certainly didn't seem to care, and he hadn't mentioned it. The only thing he seemed to care about was her safety. That definitely earned him some points.

After drying off and changing into a comfortable yellow and white striped shorts pajama set, she went in search of Luke. The floor from her bedroom down the hallway chilled her bare feet all the way to her core. It wasn't just the tile though, his whole place had a sterile feel to it. Very unlived in. The hallway opened up into a huge open room, connecting the living room and kitchen. Almost like a loft.

Modular style couches surrounded a similarly styled coffee table. There were no books or magazines and no family pictures. A couple Renoir prints hung on the white walls, but that was it. The only decent thing was the view. And man, what a view it was. High, open windows looked out onto the glistening ocean.

A loud buzz sounded from somewhere and Luke appeared from the hallway entrance. His hair was damp and he wore jeans and a T-shirt. "I'll be right back. That's the food."

While he was gone she found a bottle of red wine and opened it. She poured herself a glass, but didn't for him. He had beer and little else in the state-of-the-art stainless steel refrigerator, so she wasn't sure what he'd prefer.

After a few minutes passed she gave up waiting and retreated to the balcony. The crash of the waves immediately calmed her. She took a seat on one of the cushioned chairs, leaned back, and closed her eyes.

She turned at the sound of the sliding glass door. "I thought I might find you out here." Luke balanced one paper bag, two plates, utensils, and a beer.

Just the sight of him and her heart rate increased considerably. It didn't seem to matter that she was confused, her body sure as hell wasn't. It knew exactly what it wanted. Luke in her bed. And possibly in her life. Those were the kind of thoughts that could only lead to trouble so she brushed them aside and stood to help him. "Do you mind eating out here?"

He shook his head and started arranging the food on the circular glass table.

When they finally sat down, she had to ask, "Did you

just move in?"

He shook his head and placed an egg roll on his plate. "No. I know my condo is bare. I basically went to IKEA and bought already set up rooms."

"Seriously?" She couldn't imagine that. Her home was her safe haven, where she relaxed after weeks on the road.

Luke shrugged. "I'm never here."

She scooped sweet and sour chicken and a couple of egg rolls onto her plate and dug in. She hadn't been able to keep much down the past couple days, but she was going to make up for it now.

Caribbean music drifted up from somewhere down the beach, and the steady crash of the ocean pounded against the sand. Other than that, they ate in relative silence for the next twenty minutes.

When they were both done, she started to clear the table but he stopped her with a strong hand on her forearm. When it slid to clasp her hand, tingles shot down to her toes at the touch so she sat back down. She hated that he affected her so much, but she also didn't pull away from him. Doing that would be almost impossible. It seemed all he had to do was lightly touch her and she melted. Something she definitely didn't plan to tell him. He'd use it to his full advantage.

"I don't know what changed, but I want to clear the air." There was a slight edge to his voice. One she'd never heard before and she didn't know what to make of it.

Her throat clenched and she just nodded instead of responding. If he said something along the lines of what they'd had was fun, but it wasn't going to happen again or worse, he thought it was a mistake, she might die of embarrassment. Her original intention might have been to have something casual, but that didn't mean she wanted him voicing the same thing.

"I know things happened really fast between us and there's still a lot we don't know about each other, but that doesn't mean we can't get to know each other. For the record, I'm not interested in a one night stand." He linked his fingers with hers and it didn't feel like he planned to let go.

"Oh." Not the most appropriate response, but she was at a total loss for words.

Thankfully, he continued. "I don't expect anything from you now. I know there's still a lot going on that we're trying to figure out, but I'm not interested in anything casual...I guess I just thought you should know."

Though her hand was still linked with his, she got up and walked around the table, sat in his lap, and kissed him. It was meant to be light, reassuring, but the simple action got her blood pumping. Heat immediately pooled between her legs as his hands slid over her hips and came to rest at her waist. His hands flexed once in such a possessive manner it made her inner walls clench with a need she couldn't deny. Being so close to him—kissing him—made the most primal part of her once again wake up and take notice of Luke in a way that scared her.

After a few seconds, he pulled back. "There's one more thing—"

She placed a finger over his lips and shivered as memories of his talented mouth played in her mind. "Are you married?"

He shook his head.

"A convicted felon?"

He chuckled and shook his head again. "No, but—"

"Then it can wait until tomorrow."

Luke actually seemed relieved at her statement. Which was perfect. She didn't want to talk right now. It was overrated as far as she was concerned anyway. What she wanted was to feel Luke's very talented mouth all over her body and his thick, hard cock rock into her until they were both completely spent. If they were making love she wouldn't have to worry about the future or her growing feelings for the man currently running his hand up underneath her dress.

Chapter 10

Hope stretched and kicked the sheets off herself. Luke's bathroom door was ajar and she could hear the sound of running water. She slid out of bed and slipped on one of his button up shirts. She could have put her pajamas back on, but she loved the way he smelled. Spicy and masculine and so very sexy it made her ache in the best possible way.

She knocked on the door once before poking her head in. "Do you want me to make a pot of coffee?"

The shower curtain flew back and his grin was pure masculine hunger as he raked a gaze over her. "Sure…do you want to join me in here after?"

She glanced at his half aroused cock and flushed as it began to lengthen. It was so tempting, but… "No. You said you wanted to talk this morning and I need you to take me to the Santiagos' house. I've got to get my gear, and—"

"All right, all right. You're bad for my ego," he grumbled, but she didn't miss the teasing note in his voice.

"You're so full of it. After we get everything out of the way this morning, maybe we'll take a little trip back *here*."

His eyes lit up before he pulled the curtain back into

place.

She would have loved to join him in the shower, but now that it was morning she realized how much they needed to do. She wanted to look over her gear and make sure nothing was damaged, she needed to talk to Mac, and she figured it was time to come clean about who was after her. How she was going to tell Luke without giving away Mac's secrets, she still hadn't decided, but things had shifted between them and she needed to be honest.

It took a few minutes, but she found what she needed to make coffee. The coffee maker was the only machine in his kitchen that looked used. Everything else might as well have had price tags still attached to them.

As she pulled down two mugs from one of the cabinets, she heard the sound of rattling keys from the front of the condo. Then the unmistakable sound of the door opening and closing.

Panic seized her throat. She grabbed a knife from the knife block, but her grip loosened when a female voice starting shouting. It got louder and closer, but Hope wasn't sure what to do. She couldn't get back to Luke's room without being seen. "Luke! I saw your truck in the garage so you better get out here right now. If you think you can ignore my calls then you shouldn't have given me your security code. You won't believe what mom's gotten into. She's got some man at the house—"

The voice stopped abruptly and so did Hope's heart. A woman stood in the entrance of the kitchen. A woman who was her mirror image. Well maybe not exactly, but damn close.

Hope stared into a pair of pale blue eyes identical to her own. Her heart pounded unevenly against her ribcage and she dropped the knife. She was aware of the clatter against the tile, but couldn't drag her eyes away from the woman in front of her.

The woman's eyes had also widened and she dropped her purse, scattering the contents everywhere. Something hit Hope's foot, but she didn't look down. The woman took a few steps across the tile, but paused and wrapped her arms around herself.

Hope finally found her voice. "Who are you?"

The woman's mouth opened and shut once before she answered. "Maria…who are you?"

"Hope." She felt behind herself and clutched the counter as she spoke. Her legs shook violently so she locked her knees. She wasn't sure how much longer she could stand.

"Something smells good." Luke's voice carried down the hall.

Her throat wouldn't work. Apparently neither could Maria's.

Her eyes automatically shifted to Luke when he entered the room.

"Oh shit," he muttered as he glanced between the two of them.

A sense of rage overtook any of her shock. His reaction wasn't one of alarm. He'd known about this! "Why didn't you tell me about this?" Her voice raised a few octaves but she couldn't stop herself.

He spread his hands out in a placating manner and there was no doubt as to the apologetic tone of his voice. "I told you I wanted to talk to you about something today—"

Maria interrupted with a shout. "Oh my God! Mom is right, then." She pointed a shaky finger at Hope. It wasn't an accusing gesture, but Hope pressed back against the counter. "You're…you're…"

"Will everyone please calm down for just a second?" Luke said.

Calm down? Was he serious? Something inside Hope snapped. She had no clue what was going on, a blinding headache was spreading across her skull, and her skin felt too tight. "What the hell is going on?"

Luke started to answer, but in a few steps, Maria was across the room, embracing her like they were long lost sisters. Hope tensed and tried to shift away, but the other woman wouldn't let go. She looked to Luke for help, but his eyes had a watery sheen. What the hell was wrong with him?

"Okay, if someone would please tell me what's going on here—"

Maria finally let Hope out of the death embrace and stepped back, but not enough to give her some much needed personal space. She wiped away a few stray tears. "I think you're my missing sister, Anna."

Hope looked over Maria's shoulder at Luke, expecting a scoff or smartass retort, but he stood there. Completely mute. Staring at them.

She made eye contact with the woman and smiled apologetically. "I uh, I think you're mistaken. I know we look similar, but if I was missing, I think I'd—"

"Tell her, Luke. I thought mom was crazy, but she must be..." Maria shifted her gaze from him back to Hope. "Do you know Mac Jennings?"

"How do you know my dad?" The words were out before Hope could think. She didn't want him in any trouble.

Instead of answering, Maria turned to Luke again. "Isn't there some way we can find out if she's who we think?"

Hope hated being talked about like she wasn't in the room, but she didn't comment. Her head—and her heart—hurt too much. Luke had been lying to her this whole time? But why?

"She is Anna." The words were said with absoluteness.

As if there was no room for discussion. Like he *knew*

it was true. Which was impossible. Hope stared at him, trying to read him and desperately trying to fight the confusing feelings battling inside her. His dark eyes didn't tell her anything and his face was completely unreadable.

"What?" Maria exclaimed, her voice bordering on shrill.

Hope kept her eyes on Luke.

He rubbed a hand over his face. "This is what I wanted to talk to you about, Hope. I didn't want to do it like this, but…I sent some of your belongings to be tested."

"Tested? I don't understand. You're not making any sense. My name is Hope and before that, well, before that…" The room started to spin, but she held onto the counter for support. This was a surreal nightmare.

"Listen Hope, you are the Santiagos missing daughter. I got a call late last night while you were sleeping and…" He sighed and at least had the decency to look guilty. "You and Maria have the same DNA."

"What? You're sure?" This time Maria spoke.

Hope stared at Luke, watching him closely. His expression was completely masked. She wanted to cross the distance between them and shake him. "You lied to me? You stole my DNA? I don't understand…" Her lungs shrank and she started hyperventilating.

This couldn't be happening. None of it. She bent over and clutched her knees, trying to steady her breathing, but nothing worked. How did they know her dad? Why did this woman look exactly like her? And who the hell was Anna? Her lungs wouldn't work.

She tried to suck in a breath but her throat closed up as pure panic like she'd never experience washed over her. *Breathe*, she commanded herself, but with each gasp, her throat tightened even more.

"Hope? Hope!"

She heard Luke's voice, but couldn't keep her eyes open. Her chest and arms tingled.

Then blackness swallowed her.

* * * * *

Patrick steered the twenty year old truck he'd stolen into the Coral Gables Hospital parking lot. He didn't know what was going on, but that bastard Lucas Romanov had torn out of the parking garage like Armageddon was coming.

At least the hospital parking lot was full. It would be easier to blend in. When they'd pulled under the emergency room entrance, he'd been unable to follow. He called information, then waited twenty minutes before calling the hospital.

"Coral Gables ER," a brisk sounding woman answered.

"Hi, a friend of mine just came in. I'm stuck in traffic, but wanted to make sure she was okay."

There was a brief pause. "I can't give out patient information."

"No, I understand. I'll be there in a few minutes, anyway." Politeness always won out.

The woman sighed. "What's your friend's name?"

He gripped the phone tighter. "Hope Jennings. She should have been brought into the ER."

He heard computer keys clacking. "She's here...well that's weird...Sir, she's here, but she's not in the ER anymore. I can't give you any more information."

That *was* weird. He knew for a fact that when someone was brought in to the ER, they spent twelve hours there minimum. Especially in a hospital this big. "I understand. Thank you for your time."

He disconnected, pulled his ball cap a little lower, and walked toward the main entrance. On the way in, a

Hispanic man held the glass door open for him. Patrick stepped inside and glanced around, trying to figure out the best plan of attack. He walked toward a map of the hospital but froze when he saw *her*.

Everything around him slowed. His leaden feet refused to move.

She was walking right toward him, her arm linked with an older woman's. Her exotic face was flushed and tears pooled in her eyes. His heart seized. He had nowhere to go. When they made eye contact, he expected the worst.

Instead, she half-smiled at him as she brushed by and embraced the man who had held the door open for him.

"Papa, it's her! Doctor Gonzales moved her immediately when we told him what was going on." She was practically jumping up and down like a child. The older woman didn't say anything, just clutched a rosary.

The three of them hustled down a hallway so he trailed behind, careful not to get too close. The sterile smell accosted his senses and he remembered why he hated hospitals. They smelled like sick people. And sick people were weak.

He followed the threesome down the hall, but hung back, pretending to text message on his phone. He heard snatches of the conversation, but he might as well have been invisible because they didn't acknowledge his existence. They were too wrapped up in their conversation.

From what he gathered, the girl in front of him was Maria, she was with her parents, and they were on their way to see someone named Hope.

The fact that they were going to visit someone named Hope was too much to be a coincidence.

He slipped his cell phone back into his pocket and wiped his sweaty palms on his jeans before joining them on the elevator. This was it. If he could find out her room number, he'd come back when she was alone.

He lowered his head and hurried past the room they entered, careful not to glance directly inside. If she was in there, he couldn't risk Hope seeing his face. He had the room number and that would have to be enough for now. When visiting hours were over, he'd come back and take care of her for good.

* * * * *

Luke stared out the window of Hope's hospital room, waiting for her to wake up. Mac Jennings sat next to the bed, and the Santiagos were on their way. Hope had hit her head as she passed out. The doctor said she didn't have a concussion, but he couldn't stop the terror forking through his entire body. It was like jagged lightning.

"What the hell is she wearing?" Mac's voice cut through the quiet room, as if he'd just now noticed her state of dress.

Luke turned and looked at the older man. Mac stared at him accusingly, his green eyes boring into him, as if he could see straight to his soul. Luke looked at Hope. Maria had refused to let the doctor put her in the see-through white gown. Instead she still wore his button up, long sleeve dress shirt that was two sizes too big for her. It reached her knees, making it longer than the hospital get-up. Unfortunately, it was obvious it was a man's shirt.

He cleared his throat, but held eye contact. "It's mine."

Mac's eyes narrowed, then he sat back a fraction. "If you hurt her, I'll kill you."

It wasn't a light threat, and Luke had no doubt the other man would make good on his promise. "I could never hurt her."

Mac opened his mouth to respond, but the door flew

open and the Santiago clan rushed in.

"Luke." Jose grabbed his hand, then slapped him on the shoulder. Luke knew it to be his version of a hug. The man wasn't known for his affection.

Sonja immediately went to Mac and put a reassuring hand on his shoulder. She murmured something too low for Luke to hear. Mac nodded and patted her hand. Well, that was interesting. Since when had they become friends? Jose stiffened next to him, watching his wife interact with Mac, but he said nothing.

Maria chatted incessantly to him and Jose, but seemed content that neither responded. He couldn't take his eyes off Hope for longer than a few seconds, anyway.

"Do you think we should all be in here when she wakes up?" he asked when there was a gap in the conversation.

Everyone turned to stare at him as if he'd suggested Hope was a terrorist.

"What?" Maria demanded.

"You want her to wake up alone?" Sonja gasped.

"No, that's not what I meant. She had a panic attack and hit her head—"

"I'm awake and I want you all to leave." Hope's small voice sliced through the air like a machete.

When Luke looked at her, he realized she was staring right at him. She didn't glance at anyone else, though he wished she would. Her gaze silently accused him, and there was nothing he could say to defend himself.

She had every right to be angry at him. He just hadn't counted on it affecting him so much.

"Hope—" Mac started, but she interrupted him, still not taking her gaze off Luke.

"You can stay, Mac. Everyone else out. Especially *you*." The last part was directed at him. Her words were clipped and she sounded out of breath, as if those few words were a strain.

Instead of arguing, he sighed and did as she asked. He didn't wait to see if the others would follow, but they did. Once they were all out in the hallway, Maria punched his arm.

"What did you do to her?" Maria glared at him.

"Damn it, nothing…well, nothing except have her DNA tested without telling her."

"Oh, well I'm not sorry about that." Maria crossed her arms over her chest and leaned against the wall.

"Has the press gotten wind of this?" Jose asked.

"No, and they're not going to. We'll handle this quietly." After his confirmation that Hope was indeed Anna, he'd put an immediate call in to Kyle.

Luke made a decision that he was officially taking time off from his regular duties. His job was now to protect Hope. Whether she liked it or not.

"What precautions have you taken?" Jose continued.

Luke understood his concern. Jose's family had been targeted numerous times due to their wealth, which was precisely why Maria and Sonja rarely made public appearances. Especially after Anna's kidnapping. "Kyle's taking over all day to day concerns for right now. He's going to increase security everywhere. Everyone at the house will be informed of what's going on and they'll be signing confidentiality agreements. You haven't been in the news in a while so it's not as if you're being watched by reporters or journalists. At least we won't have to worry on that front."

Jose nodded.

"Well, what are you going to be doing?" Maria snapped.

He turned to look at his childhood friend, surprised by the sudden surge of anger in her voice. "I'll be watching Hope 24/7."

"Her name is Anna," she continued, her annoyance

obvious.

Luke sighed. He knew this had to be a shock to Maria, but he wasn't worried about *her*. His only concern was Hope.

"Stop it," Sonja interjected. "Her name is Hope and that's what we'll call her. I don't want to hear any more of this. You sound like a child, Maria." Sonja rubbed her temple and mumbled something so low Luke couldn't hear.

Jose put an arm around his wife and pulled her close. He murmured into her ear before kissing her forehead.

Luke started to suggest they get coffee when the door opened up.

Mac walked out, gave him the once over, then looked directly at Sonja. "She wants to see you."

Without a word Sonja nodded and entered the room.

"What do you say we all go get some coffee?" Mac slapped Luke on the back just a little too hard to be friendly.

He gritted his teeth. "One second." He dialed one of the men he had waiting downstairs. "I need you now."

"Who was that?" Jose asked.

Mac casually stood off to the side next to Maria, but Luke didn't miss the look that told him that he and the other man were going to exchange words.

"I've got two of my guys on standby downstairs. I'm not leaving until they're up here."

"But why?" Maria asked.

He paused, deciding how much to say. It was obvious Mac knew, and something in his gut told him he'd been straight with Sonja. Apparently not everyone was up to date. "Because someone wants her dead."

Maria gasped.

Mac just narrowed his eyes, as if he thought Luke had something to do with it. Sighing, Luke looked at Hope's door longingly. If she'd just talk to him, they could smooth things out. They had to.

* * * * *

Hope adjusted her sheet as Mac left. She hated that she still wore Luke's shirt, but it was better than the hospital gown. Too bad it smelled like him. A constant reminder of how stupid she'd been to fall for his lies. She hadn't been hired because of her work. That much was obvious. Even if he hadn't been the one to hire her, he should have mentioned something about the fact that she looked *exactly* like some missing girl. Not to mention he'd stolen her DNA. The door opened seconds later and Sonja Santiago walked in.

Hope's breath hitched. She'd intentionally avoided eye contact with the woman when everyone had been in the room. Meeting her mother was something she'd never been prepared for. She'd assumed her real mother dumped her. She hadn't known the woman was still alive and…wanted her.

Sonja took a few tentative steps forward so Hope smiled and motioned with her hand. "It's okay. I didn't mean to kick you out earlier. It's just…"

"I understand." She took a seat next to the bed and grasped Hope's hand.

Her first instinct was to yank her hand away, but she didn't. A second later, Sonja dropped her hand, though. Strangely, she missed the warmth. Looking into pale eyes so similar to her own was strange and more than a little overwhelming. She had to remind herself to breathe. She swallowed so audibly she was sure Sonja heard. A few random thoughts ran through her head, but she had no idea where to start.

Thankfully, Sonja saved her. "I guess you probably have a billion questions."

Hope nodded and her throat remained impossibly

tight. Tears threatened to overwhelm her, but she refused to let them fall. Not yet. There was so much she wanted to hear and say and if she started bawling, she'd never get everything out.

"I brought some old photos and newspaper clippings. I thought maybe the pictures might help. Mac says you don't remember much before you were seven." She pulled a large manila envelope from her purse and spread everything out on the bed.

Hope picked up the first picture she saw. It was of Sonja and Jose Santiago and two little girls in matching dresses. They all stood in front of the house she'd photographed. Her heart stuttered. It was almost surreal to be staring at this picture knowing she stared at herself, but not really remembering anything. "This is in Cuba?" She didn't know why she asked the question. She'd just been there.

Sonja nodded and wiped away a couple tears. "You remember?'

"Not really. When I was there with Luke, I had a flashback, but nothing concrete." Memories had always been fuzzy in her head, but as she glanced at the photos, she realized some of her dreams made sense. She picked up one of the newspaper articles, then looked at Sonja. "What happened?" Maybe if she understood that, she'd finally fit in somewhere. Her whole life she hadn't known who she was or where she came from. What her heritage was, even.

"We still don't know, exactly. We were at that house," She pointed to the earlier photo she'd picked up, "and you just disappeared one night. We kept expecting a ransom that never came. Weeks turned into months and months turned into years. We hired so many investigators but—" Her voice broke off on a sob so Hope picked up her hand.

Hope had never been big on affection, but the action

was instinctive.

Thankfully Sonja—her mother—continued. "I still don't understand how you ended up in the United States foster system."

Hope knew Mac had told Sonja about her past—he'd told her minutes ago—and what little memories she had of ending up in the foster system, but Hope hadn't contemplated that he'd told Sonja about the rape. Something about the other woman's tone told her that Mac had done just that. All the air left her lungs, making it impossible to speak. Could he have done that?

"He told me that you were placed in the system when you were seven, but he didn't have any details before that…he also told me how he found you…." The other woman glanced away for a fraction of a second and Hope realized Mac had indeed told her everything.

"He told you what happened to me?" Hope desperately wished Mac had left that part out. She knew the rape wasn't her fault. Nothing that had happened that night had been her fault. Still, it should have been her decision to tell this woman. If she'd ever decided to. She hated having the choice taken away from her but she still couldn't muster up much anger for Mac. He'd just had his world turned upside down too.

She nodded. "Yes, but no one else knows."

"Not even your husband?" She still couldn't think of him as being anything but a stranger. Certainly not as her father. Not yet. Maybe ever.

"No, not even your father—my husband. That's up to you, if you ever want to."

Well, that was interesting. Did Sonja keep secrets from her husband? From her tone, it was obvious she was telling the truth. Hope couldn't help but feel a small bond that Sonja was respecting her privacy.

"So why don't you understand how I ended up in foster care?"

"We didn't become American citizens until a few years after you were gone. Jose's ancestral home is in Cuba, but our real home is in Jamaica. That's where you spent your earliest years. Only recently did we move here. You'd never been to the States. It just doesn't make sense that you ended up here."

Vague memories of a dark-haired woman played in her mind. "I was found when I was seven. The woman I'd lived with died, but they couldn't find any identification, so I got put into foster care. I don't remember much about her, though, except that she told me my mother didn't want me."

Sonja gasped, and her delicate hand flew to her throat. Her pale eyes flashed a shade darker. "Never. Never in a million years would I have given you up. I can't believe...I can't believe you had to live with that lie."

The truth was apparent in Sonja's words and on her strained face. Despite what Mac had told Hope barely ten minutes ago, she hadn't known for sure if she'd ever been wanted. Couldn't have known if she'd truly been thrown away by her parents. She'd been sold by her foster father when she was fifteen to pay off his gambling debts. That was how she'd ended up on that yacht all those years ago. No one had ever wanted her until Mac.

Hope didn't trust herself to speak without crying all over Sonja.

Sonja must have understood because she continued, expertly changing the subject. "So you've been living in Florida all these years?"

Hope nodded and glanced away. The past decade she'd been trying to outrun her past. Dredging it up seemed had pointless and painful. Especially since it had nothing to do with this family. Her family, now. How was she ever going to get used to that?

Neither spoke until Sonja broke the silence. "I don't know if Mac told you, but he admitted how he saved you. I hope you know his secret is safe with us. We would never, ever put him in danger. Even if you decide you want nothing to do with our family, you must know that the sacrifices he made will always be kept safe."

Hope let out a breath she hadn't realized she'd been holding. "Thank you."

"Also…" Sonja spread her hands out in a helpless manner. "We're not going to rush things or try to force anything on you. We want you to spend some time with us, but on your own schedule."

Hope stared at the woman, then looked down at her hands. If she stared at her mother too long, she felt those damn tears well up again. She had a mother, a father, and a sister. A twin sister, at that. She couldn't believe it. Any moment she expected to wake up and realize it was all a dream.

At this point she wasn't sure if it was a good dream or a nightmare. Her life was quiet and simple.

She liked it that way.

"Do you have any questions for us?" Sonja's voice interrupted her thoughts.

Hope asked the first thing that popped into her head. "Why did you hire me?"

Sonja didn't pause in her answer. "I saw your picture on a website."

So that's how that bastard had found her. Hope's agent had started promoting her site worldwide. Maybe it had only been a matter of time before she'd been found. She chewed on her bottom lip, trying to sort everything out.

"I hope that's okay. I didn't want to just—"

Guilt assaulted her at Sonja's wide eyes. "No, of course it's fine. I was thinking how small the world really is."

Sonja took her hand again and rubbed tiny circles on her palm, as if she were afraid Hope would run away at any moment. "It's just so hard to believe you're real," she murmured.

"I know." This time Hope allowed herself to stare at the woman who had given birth to her. She drank in the delicate lines of her face and pale blue eyes. Even without the DNA test, Hope would have known this was her mother. Her whole life she thought she'd been unwanted.

A sob broke free, and for the first time in years, she let herself cry with abandon. She didn't hold anything back. She wanted to, but it was impossible. Her body demanded a release she'd never given it. Without a word, Sonja slipped into the bed with her and cradled her head against her chest. Hope cried and cried until she had nothing left. Pain and agony seeped out of her as her mother gently rubbed her back and murmured soothing words Hope could barely hear above her own wrenching cries.

Eventually, *blessedly*, she fell asleep on the chest of a woman who, hours ago, Hope hadn't known existed.

Chapter 11

Hope slipped on the simple white T-shirt and jeans Maria had brought earlier. It should feel weird wearing someone else's clothing, but they fit her perfectly. Well, almost. They were a little loose, but not much. She still felt shaky, but nowhere near passing out. She opened the bathroom door and peeked out.

Mac sat in a chair next to the bed, worry lines etched deep in the grooves of his suntanned face.

"Don't do that." She stepped out, letting the door close behind her.

"Do what?" He looked up, but his expression didn't change.

"Frown like that. I don't like it when you worry." She perched on the edge of the bed.

"Too much is happening too fast."

"Tell me about it," she mumbled.

"So what's going on with you and Luke?" He not-so-covertly glanced at Luke's folded shirt on the made bed, then raised his eyebrows at her.

"Damn. I was hoping to skip this conversation."

He held up his hands. "Hey, if you don't want to talk about it—"

"No, it's fine. There's not much to say, though. I don't know what's going on with us, especially now."

Her heart was torn in so many different directions. He'd slept with her even though he'd had suspicions about her identity and he'd stolen her DNA. She gritted her teeth thinking about his betrayal. Sure, she'd kept a secret from him, but nothing that could hurt him. She'd never been a violent person, but the thought of punching him brought a smile to her face.

"Just be careful with him. I don't want you getting hurt." Mac's tone was even, but he sounded distant. She hated that it felt like he was pulling away from her.

"I know." She glanced at the wall clock. Ten until seven. Sonja had said they'd be back to pick her up at seven thirty exactly and Hope doubted they'd be late. They wanted her to spend the next week with them, though they hadn't put any pressure on her. They just wanted to get to know her. Not that she could blame them, but spending a week with strangers who would no doubt have hundreds of questions left her feeling queasy. She needed Mac with her more than she'd admit. "Are you sure you won't stay with us?"

Mac shook his head. "No. You need to spend time alone with them and I...I need to take care of some things."

Panic rose in her throat. "You promised."

"Not that. I'm going to contact Howard and figure out how we can change your name without—"

"Wait a minute! I'm not changing my name." She couldn't keep the incredulousness out of her voice. He was her family. She'd never stop needing him. How could he not know that?

"You don't want to at least change your last name?" He shifted in his seat, but didn't break their eye contact.

She shook her head. Even if she wanted to, which she didn't, she couldn't do that. Not to Mac. She was a Jennings and always would be.

He nodded, but didn't look convinced. "Well, if you

change your mind, you won't hurt my feelings."

"Mac. You're my family. Just because they're my blood doesn't change anything. Okay, that's not true. A lot of things will change, but we won't. Not ever. You gave me back my life and whether you like it or not, you'll always be number one. Everyone else is a distant second." She couldn't believe he was worried about that. She'd never known she had family so it wasn't as if she'd had pipe dreams about being reunited with them.

He shrugged and glanced away, but she didn't miss the sheen in his eyes. She almost forgot to breathe when she saw that. She couldn't remember seeing Mac cry. Like ever.

Before she could stop herself she flung herself at him and wrapped her arms around his neck. He might not be big on affection either but he returned her embrace with equal strength, squeezing her until it was hard to breathe. But she didn't care.

As his grip started to loosen, shouting from outside the room pulled them apart. They both stood and rushed to the door.

Mac flung open the door and tried to block her, but she wiggled past him. Luke, two other men she knew worked for his security company, and a man with a red vest and a hat that said 'Gemma's Florist' were arguing.

"What's going on?" She directed her question at Luke even though she wanted to ignore him for the time being.

"Nothing." He grabbed the flower box away from the delivery man. "You can go now," he said pointedly to the man who all but ran down the hall.

"What is that?"

"It's not important." He tried to hand the box to one of the other men but she intercepted and snatched it away.

When he tried to pull it back, she knocked the box to

the floor. A dozen black roses scattered across the white tile. The garish contrast against the floor and the hateful meaning burned a hole in her gut.

"Are those for me?" she whispered.

The expression in Luke's eyes gave her all the answer she needed.

When he didn't answer Mac put a supportive arm around her shoulders. "Did it come with a card?"

Luke sighed and handed it to her. "Yeah."

Go home. You don't belong here.

Bile rose in her throat. This card couldn't have been from Taylor. It didn't make sense. "Who could have written this?"

"I don't know, but I'm going to find out." Luke's menacing tone left her with no doubt that he would. His protectiveness threw her off kilter. How could he act like that yet have lied so much to her?

A shiver snaked down her spine. The Santiagos seemed to want her to stay with them. Or she thought they did. Why would they have invited her to stay with them if they didn't?

"It wasn't any of them." Luke's deep voice cut into her thoughts, as if he'd read her mind.

She ignored him and glanced up at Mac. He didn't need any more to worry about. "Why don't you get out of here? I'm sure this will be sorted out."

He glanced back and forth between her and Luke. His jaw clenched when he stared at the other man, but his gaze softened when he returned to meet hers. "I'm not leaving town until you do and I'll have my cell phone on 24/7. Call me for anything."

Part of her was surprised he hadn't argued to stay, but she knew him better than anyone. He was planning something or he wouldn't have left her side. After he dropped a quick kiss on her head, he motioned to Luke to follow him.

She rolled her eyes. *Subtle.*

About three doors down from her room they stopped. It was too far for her to hear anything, but whatever it was, neither man looked pleased when they walked away. Something told her Mac was planning to find Patrick Taylor on his own. He might have promised he wouldn't do anything, but she doubted it. It was in his nature to take matters into his own hands. Not that he would have told Luke that. No, Mac probably threatened Luke's life or at least threatened him with bodily harm. Hope suppressed a smile at the thought.

She went back in the room to grab Luke's shirt and her purse, then changed her mind and decided to wait for the Santiagos in the privacy of her room. Seconds later, however, Luke disrupted her solitude.

"What do you want?" She crossed her arms over her chest and sat on the edge of the bed.

"I'm taking you to the Santiagos' house."

"I thought they were picking me up."

"They were, but after this you're not going anywhere without me." He stood with his feet spread a foot apart, looking like he was ready to take on a charging bull.

Which was kind of what she felt like at the moment.

She blinked and stood suddenly as his words sank in, dropping her purse and his shirt to the floor. "What the hell are you talking about?"

"I don't know what's going on and until we do, I'm your shadow." One dark eyebrow lifted in challenge.

Anger rushed through Hope with hurricane like intensity. She gritted her teeth. Now he thought he could tell her what to do? "Now wait just one minute—"

He retrieved the fallen items from the floor and tucked them under his arm. "Whatever your feelings are about me don't matter right now. You're in danger, Hope, so put your pride away."

"Why, you—"

He cut her off again. "Come on, we're getting out of here. I don't want you out in the open longer than necessary." Luke held open the door and looked at her expectantly.

Every part of her wanted to argue—and to make him argue back—but the quicker they left the hospital, the sooner she'd be able to get some space between them. Having the Santiagos as a buffer would come in handy.

She followed Luke down the hall, and the two extra bodyguards trailed behind her. Luke waited until an elevator emptied out, then she entered with him and the two other men. They boxed her in so she could barely move two inches. Despite her desire to completely ignore him, she couldn't help the tingles that shot through her at his proximity.

"Is this really necessary?" She directed her question to Luke.

He didn't look at her when he answered. "Yes."

"What about my clothes and other stuff?" She certainly didn't want to take a side trip to his place.

"I've already had everything delivered."

The rest of the walk was silent. One of the men picked them up in the front of the hospital and to her annoyance, she shared the back seat with Luke.

"I didn't mean for any of this to happen, Hope," he said quietly.

"You could have been honest with me," she snapped and continued staring out the window.

"Just like you were honest with me about who wants you dead?"

She whipped her head around to face him. "What's that supposed to mean?" He couldn't know, could he?

"It isn't Richard Taylor who wants you dead, it's his son." It wasn't a question.

"How do you know?" She couldn't believe Sonja had lied to her.

"That day in Jamaica, I saw you get sick through the window. When I saw the man on the computer screen I put everything together. I had my partner run his records...he hurt you, didn't he?" His voice was low, soothing.

A mixture of relief and sadness welled up inside her that he already knew. She swallowed and looked at her hands, but found her voice. "Yeah."

"How old were you?"

She swallowed once then found her voice. "Fifteen." When she looked back up she saw the one thing she never wanted to see from anyone. Especially not from Luke.

Pity.

Luke's hand on her thigh forced her to face him again. "What?"

"We're going to stop this guy. I promise." There was a dangerous glint in his charcoal eyes and she was glad it wasn't meant for her.

"It doesn't matter. There's a statute of limitations on rape in Florida." She balled her hands into fists. If she'd known her attacker's name back then, things might have turned out differently. Now she'd lost her chance.

"Technically you weren't a citizen—"

She cut him off. "Whatever. It's just my word against his and there's no DNA evidence. Taking him to court wouldn't do any good." Talking about this with him, of all people, wasn't something she could handle. Not now. Maybe not ever.

"I wasn't talking about prosecuting him."

Oh. She looked at him sharply and realized that he'd have no problem killing the man who had hurt her so badly she still had nightmares sometimes. The thought of him wanting to protect her like that made something unexpected bloom in her chest.

But she didn't want to continue the conversation so

she changed the subject. "Are you really going to be staying at the house with us?"

He nodded and she realized he hadn't removed his hand from her leg. Maybe she should be annoyed, but his touch grounded her. Even as it made her senses go more than just a little haywire.

"What do you make of the letter?" She didn't need to specify.

"I still don't know. I don't think it's from Taylor though."

"I don't, either. It makes no sense. It was more of a threat to my being *here*. Maria seems happy I'm here...right?" She hated the obvious desperation in her voice, but if her own sister wanted her gone she might as well pack up and head to the nearest hotel.

"More than you realize. She blamed herself almost as much as..." He shook his head and glanced out the window. When he did, he squeezed her leg before removing his hand. Immediately she missed the connection.

No way. If she had to answer questions so did he. "As who?"

He turned, his eyes filled with unmistakable sadness...and *guilt?* "As me. It was my fault."

"What? You couldn't have been more than what, twelve?" Her heart twisted at the thought. Had he really been blaming himself since he was a teenager?

He shook his head. "Thirteen."

"What could you have possibly done? You were a kid, yourself." The look of raw agony on his face almost made her forget how much he'd lied to her.

"You wanted to play with me and I told you to get lost." His face was impassive, but she knew better by now. His eyes gave him away.

"So?" That's why he felt guilty? She'd expected a lot more. Like an actual reason.

His eyes widened slightly. "So, if I'd let you play with me none of this would have happened. You would have had everything you ever wanted in life and…"

"That's crazy. Maybe Maria would have been taken, instead. You can't go back and do the 'what-ifs' in life. Trust me. I don't remember any of it, anyway."

"Nothing?"

"Not really. When we were in Cuba I had a flashback, but that's it. I've always had dreams and nightmares that made no sense and now I think I know why."

"No one's ever going to hurt you again. I promise." His deep voice told her he meant what he said.

Sadly, she knew better than to believe him. She had no doubt he meant what he said, but he couldn't make a promise like that. No one could.

"So what's Jose like? He hasn't said two words to me. I can tell he loves my—Sonja—but he doesn't say much. Even to Maria." If she was going to be spending time with them, she needed all the information she could get.

"He's a hard man to know…hold on." The buzzing of his cell phone jarred the quiet interior of the car. He glanced at the caller ID before flipping it open. "Yeah…wait, what? Are you serious? No, wait until I get to the house."

"Is everything okay?" She dug her hands into the leather seat. If something had happened to any one of them because of her she'd never forgive herself.

"We're almost there."

That wasn't an answer.

Clenching her fists in her lap, Hope stared out the window. She wanted to argue with him, but couldn't see the point. Her head ached and she didn't have much energy left after the day she'd had. She leaned back in the seat and nearly gasped aloud as they pulled into a gated community. The street was lined with mansions and every lawn was perfectly manicured. Palm trees were all the same height, grass levels were the same in every yard, and every house had two stories. At least.

When they neared the end of the road she glanced at Luke as another wrought iron gate opened up for them. Of course it was the biggest house in the neighborhood and right on the bay. She'd known they were wealthy by their home in Cuba, but reality hadn't set in until now. She hadn't even really cared because they were just employers back then. These people—her family—were loaded. How would she ever fit in? "This is where they live?"

"Yes." His answer was distracted.

As soon as they parked, the driver jumped out, and Luke turned to her. "Marcus will show you to your room. I need to take care of some things." He motioned to the man still sitting in the passenger seat.

Before she could respond, Luke got out, but instead of going in the front door, he disappeared around the side of the house.

"Hi, I'm Marcus. I know we haven't been formally introduced." The quiet blond giant from the front seat turned around and shook her hand.

"Did you used to play football?" She didn't mean the words to come out so rudely, but the man had to be at least six foot five without an inch of fat on him. His shoulders spanned much larger than the front seat. And he looked very familiar.

Instead of being offended, he chuckled. "Yes ma'am. I played in college and for a few years in the pros until I shattered my ankle. Are you ready to go inside?"

The kind, almost formal way he asked her let her know everyone who worked for the Santiagos had probably been prepped about the situation. She glanced out the back window. The driver was already rolling her bags in. "As ready as I'll ever be. You know what, I'll find the room myself." She opened the door and jumped out.

"Wait, I don't think—"

Ignoring his protests, she sprinted around the side of the house, following Luke's path. She hurried down a stone path around the palatial home until she heard voices. Very loud, angry voices. She recognized all of them. It was Jose, Sonja, Maria, and Luke. The sound of Marcus running behind her caused her to turn.

She held up a finger to her mouth. Surprisingly, he nodded and stood next to her. He didn't look happy, but at least he didn't argue.

Hovering by the edge of the house, she didn't round the corner. Whatever was going on, she wasn't going to be kept in the dark.

"What do you expect me to do? This is our livelihood!" The words came from Jose. So far she'd heard him utter only a few complete sentences.

"This is your daughter so don't use that livelihood crap on me. You have more money than you'll ever need. Send someone else!" Maria's voice raised a few octaves above his.

He never had time to respond because Sonja started shouting in a foreign language. It wasn't Spanish, Hope was sure. She guessed it was…Pashtu? What the heck was the Afghani language? She shook her head as she realized she didn't know much about her own culture. Despite the continued shouting, she couldn't help but smile.

She finally knew where she came from. What her heritage was.

"Is this normal?" she whispered to Marcus.

His lips curved into a small smile as he shrugged, then glanced away, scanning the yard and house. That private little smile of his told her a lot.

After a few minutes, their yells died down so she announced her presence. She couldn't hide forever. All four of them stood in a circle next to an Olympic-size pool. Sonja spotted her first, and quickly batted away a few tears.

"I thought you were getting settled in." Luke's voice had an accusing note to it as she walked up.

Before she could respond, he waved behind her so she glanced back. Marcus stood by the edge of the house, but when Luke gave him the go-ahead, he disappeared.

She shrugged and walked toward them until she stood in between Sonja and Luke, facing the others. "What's going on?"

"Nothing," Maria mumbled and averted her gaze.

She glanced at all of them. Maybe it was none of her business but she didn't want to be the cause of any trouble between them. "It doesn't sound like nothing."

Jose sighed. "I'm so sorry, but I must go to Costa Rica on business. We have—"

"You don't have to go, you could send someone else," Maria's voice held an edge of something Hope couldn't put her finger on. It was more than anger. Disappointment maybe?

He ignored Maria and looked back and forth between Hope and Sonja, but mainly he looked at Sonja. That's when Hope realized he wasn't apologizing to her specifically, but to his wife for leaving. He might love his wife, but he wasn't going to win father-of-the-year anytime soon.

"It's fine. Seriously, go." Everyone stared at her so she shrugged. "What? If it's that important, go."

It stung Hope that she'd been missing for so long and he couldn't figure out a way to stay and get to know his long-lost daughter, but part of her didn't care. She had Mac and no one could compare to him.

"Thank you for understanding. There have been many fires and I can't leave this to someone else. I should be back within a week." He took a step forward, as if he might hug her, then changed his mind and retreated inside.

"We'll talk in a little while. I need to speak to him before he leaves." Sonja cupped Hope's face and kissed her on the cheek. As she walked away, Hope didn't miss the raw hurt in her eyes.

Maria rolled her eyes once they'd both gone. "He's never going to change."

"Give him a break," Luke mumbled, but even Hope could tell he didn't mean it.

"Why should I? He's never been there for me. I don't know why I thought he'd be different with my sister." Maria met Hope's gaze. "You're lucky you have Mac. He obviously has priorities."

Hope nodded and tried to ignore the pain she experienced when witnessing the emotion in Maria's eyes.

She wasn't sure how to respond to her twin. Comforting others wasn't something she was used to. Maria might have had everything money could buy growing up, but she obviously hadn't had her father's love. Strange that it was the only thing Hope did have. Mac would always be her dad. No matter what changed in her life. That wouldn't.

Luke reached out for Maria, but she shrugged away from him and headed toward the back door. At the French doors, she paused and turned. "I'm going to check on my—our mom—then maybe we can share a glass of wine?"

Hope smiled. "Of course."

"Well, now you know this isn't the perfect home," Luke murmured.

She looked up at him, and a smile tugged at her lips.

"Thank God for that." She'd been worrying how she'd fit in. They might be rich, but they had problems just like the rest of the planet. When he didn't say anything she continued. "Do they always fight?"

He shook his head and led her to two lounge chairs on the lanai. "No, but Jose has never been the doting father." He risked a quick glance toward the door and she guessed it pained him to admit his next words. "Or much of a father at all."

She'd caught that. She'd been missing for decades and he barely looked at, or, talked to her. Talk about cold. "He seems to love Sonja, though."

Luke nodded. "Sometimes I think she's the only person he does love. I guess Maria just got it into her head that things might change with you here."

"What's so important that he has to leave *tonight*?" Hope struggled to control her temper. It shouldn't bother her, but the more she thought about the situation, the harder it was to digest.

"There have been a few intentional fires at one of his biggest plantations. Security has been tighter than usual so we think it's an inside job."

"Should you be going with him?" Though she wouldn't admit it out loud, the thought of Luke leaving made something sharp twist inside her chest.

He let out a bark of laughter. "I wasn't kidding when I said I was going to be your shadow."

She chewed on her bottom lip. For some reason, the thought bothered and excited her. She was still annoyed at him, but every time he looked at her, her body simply reacted. Even now her traitorous nipples tightened under his scrutiny. The man was too sexy for his own good.

After a few moments of intense silence where it seemed he was having the same thoughts she was, he finally stood so she followed suit. "I'll show you where your room is."

"Where's your room?" She immediately wanted to bite back the question.

He raised a dark eyebrow, then leaned close, murmuring in her ear. His voice was sensual yet teasing. "I'm in the room next to yours...and my door is definitely open."

She nudged him with her hip was they walked inside. She wanted so much to be angry at him, but he was her only ally at the moment. Once inside the expansive house, she instinctively leaned closer to Luke. It had almost nothing to do with her desire for him though. Everything looked so expensive she didn't want to risk breaking anything.

After navigating down a couple hallways, they stopped in front of a plain white door. "This is your room."

"Thanks." She shifted from one foot to the other as he stared at her with that impenetrable gaze. "Listen, I uh...I have a question." If she didn't ask it would eat away at her insides.

"What is it?"

"Maybe it's none of my business, but uh, did you ever have a relationship with Maria?" She looked down at her clasped hands. Maria did have a key to his place. It's not as if they acted intimate, but she couldn't help but wonder.

He snorted. "I can't believe you asked that, but no. Never. God, no."

She stared at him, surprised by his adamant denial. "Why is that such a foreign idea? We look exactly alike."

He lightly fingered a loose strand of her hair before tucking it behind her ear. "My attraction to you has nothing to do with your face."

At that, he turned and walked the few feet to the next room.

Well, then. Her heart rate increased substantially and there was a very feminine flutter in her stomach. Didn't he know exactly the right thing to say? She was supposed to be mad at him but he was making it very hard. Sighing, Hope opened the door to her room. When she flipped on the light, all the air left her lungs in a ragged whoosh. The duvet was ripped to shreds and on the wall was written *Go Home*. Just like the letter from the hospital. She gripped the door frame and tried not to fall.

"Luke." All she could manage was his name. Her knees gave way, but before she hit the floor strong arms gripped her from behind.

"Shit," Luke muttered.

Unable to speak, she managed to turn and wrap her arms around his neck. Holding him wouldn't make what was on the wall disappear, but having his strong arms surrounding her made her feel a lot better.

"Come on. Into my room." Luke wrapped a protective arm around her and led her to his room, but he didn't stay. "Don't open the door for anyone but me."

She nodded even though the last thing she wanted was for him to leave her. She jumped when the door clicked into place behind him, but she quickly locked it. What had her life turned in to? She couldn't imagine Patrick had broken into the Santiagos' home just to torment her. If he'd been here, he'd have killed her.

No, someone else hated her enough to do this.

The question was, who? And why? She knew without a doubt that it wasn't her mother. The love she'd seen in Sonja's eyes was so real it was a living, breathing thing.

If it was Maria, her sister... Hope batted away the unexpected wetness on her cheeks. She just prayed it wasn't.

151

Chapter 12

Luke shut the door behind him, pulled out his SIG, then crept down the hall toward the kitchen. Gun drawn, he entered the spacious room. Anthony, a man who'd worked with him for six years, and Marcus, who'd worked there for five, both stood and drew their guns.

"What's going on?" Marcus asked first.

"Someone's in this house. They destroyed Hope's room. Marcus, I want you guarding the room I'm in. First floor—"

"I know which one it is. Is she in there?"

"Yes. Don't let anyone go inside. *Anyone.*" He didn't know what the hell was going on, but if someone in this family—a family he considered as close as his own—was involved, they were going to pay.

He looked at the other man. "Anthony, you check the grounds. I'm going to check on everyone else."

Anthony nodded. "I'm on it. Jose left for the airport and Sonja went with him so Rico isn't here."

Rico usually drove Jose so that made sense. "So Maria's still here?"

"In her room, last I saw. And, I think Lydia's here."

Lydia was their sixty-year old cleaning lady, so he doubted she was involved. Still, he wasn't taking any chances.

"Okay, I'm gonna call Anderson in as backup," Luke said.

Everyone nodded and spread out. He called Anderson, who was only ten minutes away, then crept up the stairs toward the main rooms. Everything happening was too weird. Luke hated leaving Hope under Marcus's protection, but he had to take care of this and he trusted the other man with his life. If anything happened to Hope…no, he wouldn't think about that. He couldn't. Not if he wanted to function normally.

Stopping at Maria's door, he knocked, then opened the door.

"What the hell? You don't wait anymore?" She had on a robe and her hair was wrapped in a towel on top of her head.

In response, he put a finger to his lips and motioned for her to get back in the bathroom. Immediately she complied. They'd had a few scares before so she wasn't completely naïve.

He opened her walk-in closet and quickly surveyed it. When he pushed aside a huge stack of dresses, he tripped on a pair of beat-up tennis shoes covered in dirt. He stared at them for a moment, then made a mental note. It could mean nothing, but the dirty shoes didn't belong with her Jimmy Choo's and Manolo's.

"You can come out," he called out.

The door flung open. Maria's face had paled. "What's going on?"

"I'm not sure yet. Stay in here and don't come out for anyone. Do you still have that nine millimeter I got you last Christmas?"

She nodded and swallowed. "It's in my nightstand."

"Good. Use it if you have to. Lock the door behind me." He didn't give her a chance to argue or question.

His phone rang as he exited.

It was Anderson. "I'm here. Just saw Anthony on the

grounds."

"Good. Take the first floor. Marcus is standing guard outside Hope's door and he's not moving."

Once they disconnected, he methodically swept each room, checking closets, under beds, everywhere and anywhere possible someone could think to hide. An hour later, he reconvened with his men in the kitchen. It didn't make sense. They kept the security system off during the day, but to get past his men was unthinkable. Especially now.

"Anyone find anything?" he asked.

Everyone shook their head except Anthony. "I found footprints in the greenhouse and the system has been disabled there too."

"Did you disturb anything?"

Anthony snorted. "No, I was trained better than that."

"All right. Call the police. The room hasn't been touched so maybe they'll be able to lift some prints."

"What are you gonna do?" Marcus asked.

"I'm getting Hope and Maria the hell out of here. The police don't need to know they were here either." He looked pointedly at both men, who nodded.

Luke didn't want the women to be taken downtown for hours of questioning. Not when they couldn't answer questions, anyway. It would be a waste of time, and he wasn't going to chance letting Hope or Maria out in the open.

He sheathed his gun and pulled out his phone, hating that he had to make this call. At the rate things were happening, Hope might jump on the next plane out of here.

Jose picked up on the second ring. "Luke, is everything okay?"

"Is Sonja still with you?"

"Yes. The plane's being fueled now." His words were clipped.

Briefly, he filled him in on what had happened. "I need you to take Sonja with you."

"Done."

Luke hadn't expected much of an argument. Jose was an odd man. His love for Sonja was borderline obsessive. That's why Luke never understood that he'd never doted on Maria. She was a part of Sonja but it didn't seem to matter.

"Do you think you'll have a hard time convincing her?" he asked.

Jose sighed and Luke could picture Jose pinching the bridge of his nose. "Yes, but I'll make it happen."

"Good." After they disconnected, he rubbed his temple. If Luke thought he could force Maria to go with them too, he would. Unfortunately, he knew her temper and she wouldn't go anywhere with her father right now.

Hope was the only one he refused to let out of his sight. He'd made a promise to her and intended to keep it. He'd screwed up with her and he owed it to her. But that wasn't the only reason he wouldn't let her out of his sight. The more he was around her the more he realized what he felt for her wasn't casual.

True to form, Marcus hadn't moved from his spot as guard dog. When he saw Luke, he moved out of the way. "No one's come in or out."

"Hope?" He knocked on the door.

The door swung open and instead of being scared like he expected, her face was red with barely contained anger. "What the hell is going on?"

He ignored her anger, knowing it wasn't directed at him. "Marcus is going to take your bags and you to the car. I'll be there with Maria in five minutes." Without giving her time to argue, he hurried out of the room and back to Maria's. He would have liked to send Marcus in his place so he could stay with Hope, but when Maria was in a pissy mood, she didn't listen to anyone but

Luke. They'd grown up together and he was like a brother to her.

"Maria it's me. Let me in."

When she opened the door he couldn't contain his surprise. A half-packed suitcase was already on the bed.

"What are you doing?"

She shrugged and tossed in a pair of jeans. "I don't know what's going on, but I know we're not staying here."

"How much longer do you need?" He checked his watch.

"Sixty seconds." She grabbed two pairs of sandals from the closet, then rushed to the bathroom. True to her word, a minute later her bag was zipped.

He pulled the luggage off the bed and she grabbed her toiletry bag.

"Where are we going?"

"My place."

"Now can you tell me what's going on?" she asked as they descended the stairs.

"Someone ransacked Hope's room."

"What?" Her voice shook and she stopped on the stairs until he took her arm, prodding her to continue.

"It looks like someone disabled the security through the greenhouse. We don't know who could have done this, but the police are on their way."

Maria's face paled and something flared in her eyes. Guilt? He couldn't be sure. It happened so quickly, then it was gone and he couldn't be sure he hadn't imagined it. His gut clenched. Maria couldn't be involved with this. Little surprised him about human nature anymore, but she'd been so excited her sister had been found it didn't seem feasible.

"Shouldn't we wait until they get here?" Her question interrupted his scrutiny of her.

He shook his head. "No, I want to get you both out of

here." Technically and legally he knew they should wait, but he didn't want Hope exposed, and he definitely didn't want her taken down to the police station.

Once they reached the four-door garage, Maria slid into the backseat with Hope and he took the front.

"Are you okay?" Maria took Hope's hand and squeezed it.

Hope looked uncomfortable, but she didn't pull away. "I guess." She met his gaze and he didn't miss the untrusting look in her eyes. Hope didn't trust any of them. It was obvious. Hell, he was surprised she was still in town.

* * * * *

Patrick shifted in the cab of his truck, waiting across the street for Hope and her 24/7 bodyguard to return. She'd already checked out when he'd gone back to the hospital. Now he had no clue what to do. He assumed they'd return to the condo. If they didn't, he had to leave the country, but he couldn't without knowing she was dead.

Leaning back against the headrest, he almost dozed off when his phone vibrated across the center console. He snatched it up. "Yeah?"

It was his contact. "I've got what you want."

"All right. Who are they?"

"I got this from a nurse at the hospital. The girl, Hope Jennings, had all her hospital bills paid by a man named Jose Santiago."

"Who's he?"

"Jose Santiago provides about half of the coffee to the world."

"I've never heard of him." That was odd. He thought he knew every major player in the financial world.

"Neither had I, so I ran a detailed search. About

twenty-three years ago, one of his children was kidnapped. Her name was Anna and she was never found."

His gut roiled. "Was she a twin?"

"You guessed it."

It made sense. The woman at the hospital had to be Hope's sister.

The other man continued. "The family keeps pretty much to themselves. They're wealthy, but they don't flaunt it. They pay taxes, donate to charity, and attend church. Maria, the other daughter, works in real estate. She's got a hand in a lot of Miami high-rises. Basically, they're hard-working citizens who keep to themselves."

A plan formed in his mind. If he could get to Hope's sister, he could force her out from her constant protection. "Does this Maria girl work by herself?"

"No, she's got a partner...David Dubois."

"Can you look up his info for me?"

"Already have." He rattled off the man's address and information.

Patrick noted everything and took another antacid. He couldn't wait until this mess was over. The sooner he got out of the country, the better.

"I talked to your father's attorney." The words caught him off guard.

"Yeah, so?" Screw his father. The man would have sold him out for a hand job.

"The Feds haven't gotten to questioning him about the contract on Hope, but they have hinted about it."

"What does that have to do with me?" He started the engine to his truck and pulled out of the parking lot.

The other man let out a sharp bark of laughter. "If you don't get your father's *special* passport and extra money to his attorney, he assures me it will very much be your problem."

"And if I don't? Will this affect our arrangement?"

He'd already paid the man so there wasn't much he could do if it did.

"No. I'm just the messenger. You paid me and I don't negate on a deal."

For some reason, his words weren't comforting.

They disconnected as Patrick steered into traffic. He needed to find an all night internet café. Map-questing David Dubois's address shouldn't be too difficult.

* * * * *

Hope rolled over and glanced at the clock. It was close to midnight and she still couldn't sleep. They'd been at Luke's for over an hour, but her heartbeat hadn't returned to normal. In her gut she couldn't believe Maria had written on the wall, but who else could it have been? Maria had wanted to hang out and chat when they'd arrived at Luke's, but Hope had feigned a headache.

Luke hadn't believed her excuse, though. She'd seen it in his eyes. At least he didn't say anything or try to get her to stay. Kicking off the sheets, she got out of bed. She itched to call Mac, but she couldn't put all this on him, too. He'd been through enough and even though she didn't completely trust Luke, she trusted him enough to figure this out and to protect her.

If he'd managed to figure out what happened with Patrick Taylor, she had no doubt he'd figure this out, too. Seconds later, she stood in front of Luke's bedroom door. When she'd gotten out of bed, she hadn't planned to see him. Her feet apparently had a mind of their own.

She raised her hand to knock, but the door flew open. "How'd you know I was here?"

"I saw the shadow of your feet." He pointed down, but his eyes never left hers.

Without his shirt on, she had a hard time focusing on

his face and not his bare chest. She bit her bottom lip, not sure what she wanted, but unwilling to walk away.

At least he didn't ask. Instead he stood back, and motioned with his hand that she could come in.

Tentatively, she sat on the edge of his bed. "I didn't...I don't want to be alone tonight." Sex was the last thing on her mind. Even if he did look good enough to eat, her thoughts wouldn't settle down.

"You can stay here. No pressure." His smile was wry as he lifted his hands in a placating gesture.

Yeah right. Without a word she slipped under the covers. He switched off the lamp, but left the bathroom light on. The small crack illuminated the room just enough so she could see him walking toward the bed.

He slid in next to her, pulled her back against his chest and just held her. She could feel his erection and the erratic beat of his heart, but he never made a move.

For that she was grateful. Her thoughts about him were still in limbo. He'd broken her trust, yet at the same time, she felt safe near him. Having sex with him might push her over the edge into dangerous emotional territory.

All her emotions were right at the surface. Any more complications and she was likely to have a mental breakdown. How she wished she could go back to her normal life in The Keys, when the most she worried about was getting sunburned.

"What are you thinking about?" he murmured in her ear, his deep voice sending a delicious thrill down her spine.

"How complicated my life has become." *Including my involvement with you.*

He pulled her tighter, his arm a steel band of reassurance. "We'll fix this. I promise."

We? She didn't comment. "Who do you think did this?"

"I'm not sure. It's possible Taylor sent those flowers and broke into the house using the greenhouse as an entrance, but…" He sighed.

"But, it just doesn't make sense," she finished for him.

"Exactly," he spoke low in her ear, causing heat to pool between her legs.

She ignored it. Or rather she tried to. She shifted, trying to move away from the feel of his erection, but it was impossible.

He chuckled. "Sorry about that. I can't be in the same bed as you and not…" His hand strayed from its position around her waist to rest on her hip.

He played with the elastic of her pajama bottoms, tracing his finger along the ridge until his hand slipped under. Her breath caught when she realized what he was doing. She should stop him, but the words stuck in her throat.

He paused, presumably waiting for her to tell him to stop. When she didn't, he slipped his hand under her panties until his hand was over her mound. Touching and teasing.

She opened her mouth, but all that came out was a gasp.

"Do you want this?" He nipped her neck, and she jerked under his touch.

"Do you plan on using sex to get what you want all the time?" Her words were strangled. It was a wonder she could talk at all.

He chuckled and turned her on her back, but kept his hand between her legs. "I'll do anything to keep you in my bed."

What about your life? The unbidden thought popped into her head, but she willed it away. This was about sex. Nothing more.

Right. Keep telling yourself that. The voice in her

head was silenced when his mouth covered hers. All the warning bells and words of caution dissipated, but she knew they'd be back in the morning. Right now, however, nothing else mattered but what she and Luke could make each other feel.

Chapter 13

Hope opened her eyes and stifled a groan. Luke lay on his back, his breathing deep and steady. Quietly, she found her pajamas and slipped them back on. She was a little sore, but the pleasure had been worth it. Maybe she should feel bad or guilty, but for a few hours, he'd been able to make her forget everything.

She stared at him for a moment while he slept. Of all people, why did she have to fall for him? Shaking her head, she slipped out of his room. The fresh aroma of coffee immediately hit her senses so she ventured to the kitchen.

"Morning." Maria was pouring herself a mug when Hope walked in.

"Good morning. Did you talk to…Sonja? Did they make it safe?" She wondered if she'd ever be able to think of Sonja as her mother without pausing.

Maria glanced down and cleared her throat. "Sure."

"You're probably the worst liar I've ever met," Hope muttered.

Maria looked up and grimaced. "Sorry. I talked to her last night and she didn't go with him."

"What?" Luke was going to be pissed when he found out. Not that Hope particularly cared. But she was worried about Sonja's safety.

"She made me promise not to tell Luke, so you have to also."

Luke had lied to her on more than one occasion. It should be easy enough. So why did she feel so lousy? "She's not at your house, is she?"

"Of course not. She's actually staying at the same hotel with Mac. She said they have adjoining rooms."

"Really?" Well that was certainly interesting. Adjoining rooms? Whatever Mac was planning, she didn't want him involving Sonja. Not that she thought he would. So why were they hanging out?

Damn, she missed her uncomplicated life.

"Yep, she's meeting us for brunch today." Maria shrugged. It struck Hope as odd that Maria wasn't concerned.

"Brunch?" She poured herself coffee and added a little sugar.

"Oh, sorry. I told her we'd both be there. I hope that's okay." Maria glanced over her shoulder at her as she pulled creamer from the refrigerator.

"No, it's fine. More than fine." Spending uninterrupted time with them should be nice. Now that she'd had a chance to sleep on it, she wasn't as worried about Maria being involved with trashing her room. It didn't make any sense. Hope had spent a lifetime mistrusting everyone. Until she could prove anything or until her gut told her otherwise, she'd made up her mind to give her sister the benefit of the doubt.

"So, you and Luke, huh?" Maria raised her eyebrows and leaned against the counter as she took a sip of her coffee.

Hope felt heat creep up her neck and face. "I don't know what we are." Inwardly she groaned. She hadn't even had a full serving of caffeine and Maria wanted to talk about this?

Her sister smiled. "I'm glad."

She took a sip of her drink, but didn't respond.

The disbelief must have been evident on her face because Maria continued, "It's about time he dated someone normal. Besides, if you two get married, then he'll be my brother." Her smile was genuine.

Hope nearly choked as she set her mug down on to the counter. "Married? No way. Whatever *this* is," she spread her hands out in a noncommittal gesture, "it isn't serious." Or at least she didn't think it was. She trusted him with her body, that was for sure. Anything else, she was too confused.

"Hmm." Maria shook her head knowingly.

"It's not, I swear."

"Do you want to drink this out on the balcony?" Maria lifted her mug.

Thankful for the change in subject, Hope nodded. Once they were both seated, the distant sound of the ocean was their only company. That suited Hope just fine.

After a few minutes, Maria broke the silence. "I'm sorry you had to see us fighting yesterday, especially your first day there."

"You don't have anything to apologize for." After everything she'd gone through the past week, seeing the Santiagos fight was the least of her worries. In a strange way, it was comforting.

"I think I had a vision of what it would be like if you were ever found. I thought maybe…maybe things would change," she mumbled, and stared out at the ocean.

"You mean with your father?"

Maria nodded.

"What's his deal?" Hope wasn't going to sugarcoat it. The guy was sort of a jerk.

"I don't know. Mom said he was different before you were taken, but I don't remember it ever being different. She said that after you were gone, something inside him died and he couldn't bond with me. Whatever, I'm tired of the sad excuses she makes for him." Maria leaned back in her chair and propped her bare feet up on the table where Hope and Luke had eaten two nights before.

"At least you have your mom." Hope ignored the twinge of jealousy she experienced.

Maria started to respond when Luke walked out onto the balcony carrying a steaming mug. Thank goodness he had a shirt on. He handed a cell phone to Maria. "Your phone's been ringing off the hook. I'm surprised you didn't hear it." As if on cue, the phone started ringing.

"It's barely eight. What on earth does he want?" she mumbled as she glanced at the caller ID, and walked back inside.

"How long have you been awake?" Instead of sitting next to her, Luke stood near the sliding glass door, almost uncertainly.

"Ten, maybe twenty minutes. Oh, Maria and I are having brunch with…with each other today. I'm not sure how that works into your plan, but I don't think it's up for discussion." Hope shrugged. She'd let Maria and him hash it out.

"Fine, but I'm going with you."

She'd known he'd argue and in truth, she wasn't going anywhere without him or one of his bodyguards. She wasn't stupid. "Whatever you say, but I don't think Maria—"

Maria stormed back out onto the balcony. "Luke, mom stayed in town and we're having brunch with her." She poked him in the chest then turned back to Hope. "I've got to meet my business partner. I've left all the info for the restaurant on the counter. I'll meet you around eleven?"

"Sounds good." Hope didn't move from her spot. Until she finished that first cup of coffee, she was staying put.

"Luke, you can bring her, but you're not sitting with us. This is strictly girls only." She winked at Hope and went back inside.

"Are you two ganging up on me now?" he grumbled and sat next to her.

Hope smothered a smile.

Luke mumbled something else under his breath and pulled out his cell phone. Hope listened to him and the crashing waves.

When he hung up, she didn't bother to hide the fact that she'd been listening to his conversation. "So Marcus is going to be following Maria. Does she know that?"

He shook his head, his lips curving up slightly. "No, and I plan to keep it that way. She's more stubborn than you."

"Have you heard anything about what happened at the house?"

"No. The police were there and dusted for prints, but who knows how long that'll take. I put in a call to a friend of mine and he's going to see if he can expedite the tests."

She pushed down her disappointment. Even though she understood, it still sucked. Vandalism wasn't going to make it to the top of the list of crimes to solve.

Especially not in a place like Miami.

* * * * *

Hope automatically glanced at her watch when Sonja looked at her own. It was half past eleven. They'd been at the restaurant since a little before eleven. Luke sat three tables away. Far enough away to give them privacy, but close enough to see them at all times. "Is she normally late?"

Sonja glanced around the Italian restaurant and

frowned. "No. In fact, she's normally fifteen minutes early. I'm usually the late one."

"Has she answered her cell phone?" she asked the question even though she already knew the answer.

"No. It's turned off." Worry was evident in Sonja's voice and it shredded Hope's heart.

Hope glanced around, too. The restaurant was small and cozy. A few families talked and laughed, but there was no mistake. Maria wasn't there. She couldn't temper down her growing anxiety.

She waved Luke over. As soon as he slid into the seat across from her she asked, "Have you called Marcus?"

He nodded. "Yeah, her car is still parked outside the Pink Flamingo. She probably just got caught up with the developer."

Hope chewed her bottom lip. The Pink Flamingo was where Maria had gone to meet her partner. A new highrise was being built and there had been some sort of emergency. Something to do with a leak on the top floor.

"Will you call him again and ask him to go inside and look for her?"

Luke nodded and pulled out his phone. Sonja tapped her finger on the table, obviously as worried as Hope was. A waiter approached their table, but Sonja shooed him away with a flick of her wrist. Hope knew he was annoyed with them for not ordering, but she didn't care. When everything turned out fine, she'd over tip him for taking up his table for so long.

She stood and Luke cast her a sharp look. "I'm going to the restroom," she whispered to both of them. She certainly didn't need his protection in the ladies room.

Sonja nodded distractedly and Luke just frowned as he listened to Marcus.

Once she was in the privacy of the restroom, she splashed cold water on her face and patted it dry. Maria being late had to be more than a coincidence. She didn't care what Luke thought, they had to go look for Maria themselves. Pulling out lip gloss from her purse, she smoothed some on, trying to calm her nerves. She started to leave when the ring of her phone echoed through the small room.

The number was unfamiliar, but on the off chance it was her sister, she answered. "Hello?"

"If you want to see your sister again, I suggest you do exactly as I say."

Bile rose in her throat. She recognized that voice. He certainly wasn't trying to hide who he was now. Not a good sign. "I want to hear her voice first."

He paused and she worried he wouldn't comply. "Fine." Seconds later Maria's voice was on the line. "Don't do what he says! Don't listen to the son of a—"

A loud smacking sound vibrated in her ear. It was followed by a sharp cry from Maria.

Her heart rate tripled, but she somehow found her voice. "I'll do whatever you say. Just don't hurt her."

"Meet me at the Miami Beach Marina in twenty minutes. Do you know where that is?"

"Yes." She didn't, but figured a taxi driver would.

"I'll call you in twenty minutes with further directions. Come alone and don't be late. If I see anyone with you, she's dead."

Before she could argue, he'd disconnected. Wiping sweaty palms on her jeans, Hope tried to think of a plan. She couldn't tell Luke what was going on. She knew how serious Patrick Taylor was. Instinctively, she rubbed the scar on her shoulder. Phantom pain shot through her. If he even thought he saw someone with her, he wouldn't hesitate to kill Maria. She couldn't lose the sister she'd just found.

She slipped her phone into her back pocket, then peeked out the door. The restrooms were separated from the dining area by a long hallway. There was an emergency exit at one end, but she didn't want to alert anyone that she'd left. She took a deep breath and rushed down the hall. Around the corner Luke was still deep in conversation on his phone and Sonja was looking at the main entrance.

Before she could change her mind, she hurried out of the hallway and pushed through the swinging doors to the kitchen.

"You can't be in here," a woman with a long white apron looked at her disapprovingly from a work station where she diced tomatoes.

"My ex-husband just walked in. Where's the exit?" Maybe playing the sympathy card might work.

The woman rolled her eyes and pointed around a rolling stack of bread trays. "Around there, past the dishwashers. You can't miss it."

"Thank you." She didn't need to tell Hope twice. Seconds later the bright sun hit her face. The smell of garbage and rotting food accosted her, but she didn't have time to think. She needed transportation. And fast.

An open parking lot sat right behind the restaurant. Across the lot, the street over, she spied two yellow taxis.

"There is a God," she murmured as she began sprinting.

* * * * *

Luke snapped his phone shut and fought the acid hole burning in his gut. With the exception of Maria's vehicle, Marcus hadn't been able to find signs of Maria or her partner, David. Marcus had scoured the building, but it was empty except for a couple construction workers. They hadn't seen either of them.

"Anything?" Sonja asked.

"No...where's Hope?" He glanced toward the

hallway she'd disappeared down.

Sonja glanced at her watch. "Hmm. I'll go check on her."

Moments later she was back, her face pale and drawn. "She's not in there."

He flagged down their waiter. "Have you seen the young woman who was at this table?"

The guy shrugged and pointed to the kitchen. "She ran out the back."

That's all Luke needed to hear. Instead of using the kitchen, he ran out the front door and circled around the back. From his position, he saw her across the parking lot and the adjoining street. He shouted her name, but she was too far away to hear him.

For a few seconds, she talked to a man with dreadlocks, then got into a bright yellow taxi. Panic set in. There wasn't enough time to follow them.

Sonja came up behind him. "What's going on?"

"I don't know, but there's only one reason Hope would have left without telling us." He fished his keys out of his pocket as they hurried to the car. Once they slid inside, he flipped open his cell phone and called Anthony, one of the best men who worked for him, and a computer genius.

As soon as Anthony picked up, Luke said, "Activate the tracking devices."

"Shit," Anthony mumbled. "Which ones?"

"All of them. I don't know what shoes she's wearing. I think she's got her cell phone with her, but she might get rid of it."

"Give me a sec. I've gotta fire up my laptop."

Luke tapped his finger against the steering wheel, hating the feeling of being out of control. He'd put tracking devices in all of Hope's shoes. She didn't wear much jewelry, and there was always a chance she'd take a piece of jewelry off even if she did. So, he'd done the next best thing.

"Okay. Only one of the signals is moving. It's going about forty miles per hour toward the coast."

Luke put the truck in gear and veered out into traffic. He handed the phone to Sonja. "Put him on speaker."

A second later they were both hearing the same thing. "Okay, now she's on Fifth Street heading east...she's slowing down...Okay, she made a right on Alton Road...shit, she's heading to the Miami Beach Marina."

"Damn it!" He pounded the steering wheel when they hit a red light.

"David Dubois owns a boat there," Sonja interjected.

"You're right. Anthony, look up his info, see what you can find." Something had happened to Maria. In his gut, he knew that's what was going on. He risked a glance at Sonja, wishing he could ease some of her pain. She had to know both of her daughters were in danger. The thought of losing both of them—no, Luke refused to go down that road.

"Looks like he owns a sailboat named Stargazer. Pier C, slip 20. That's on—"

"Yeah, I know what side of the marina that's on. Is she moving?" Gunning the engine, Luke raced through a yellow light.

He heard Anthony clicking on the computer. "Yeah, but she's slowing down. Now she's moving about two miles per hour so she must be walking."

Luke took a sharp left and sped up. He was almost there. That bastard Patrick Taylor had to have taken Maria. And probably her partner by the look of things. Maria wouldn't have disappeared without a reason and he knew Hope wouldn't have just left without saying goodbye. She might be stubborn, but she wasn't stupid.

As they pulled into the gravel parking lot, he shot a look at Sonja. "Stay in the car."

Sonja nodded, but for some reason he didn't quite

believe her.

"I'm serious, I can't find her if I'm worrying about you."

"I promise I'll stay here." She clutched her cell phone in her lap, and something told Luke she was planning something, but there wasn't a damn thing he could do about it. Hope and Maria were his priorities.

He kicked the truck into park, but left the keys in the ignition. "Anthony you still there?"

"I'm here buddy."

"Good. Hold on a sec…Sonja, call the police if I'm not back in thirty minutes."

He wasn't sure what she'd tell them, but if he couldn't find Hope, he wanted the entire marina ripped apart.

Phone still in hand, Luke jumped out of the truck. "What's she doing now?"

"According to the map on the marina website, and the info I have on Dubois, it looks like she's nearing his slip. I think you're right. That's where she's going. Do you need backup?"

"Yes, send Rico now. If we don't have to involve the police until after we have them back I'd prefer it."

"You're not bringing this guy in alive, are you?"

"What do you think?" He didn't answer outright because one never knew who was listening, but bringing Patrick Taylor in alive had never been part of the plan. Not after what he'd done to Hope.

Chapter 14

Hope stared at the face of the man who'd caused her so many nightmares and years of therapy. It was weird, but he didn't seem as terrifying as she remembered. Of course, she'd been a scared fifteen-year-old girl back then. His face made her want to vomit, but the pain she'd dealt with for so long wasn't there. It didn't sit leaden in her gut anymore. Talk about shock therapy.

"Take a seat over there with your sister," he said the last word as a sneer. He pointed in the direction with his gun.

As if she didn't know where he meant. Maria sat next to a man Hope didn't recognize on the wooden settee in the kitchen area of the sailboat.

Patrick rubbed his forehead, gun still in hand. He mumbled to himself and Hope guessed he hadn't gotten much sleep in the past few days. Bags hung heavy under his red eyes, and his whole body trembled. Maybe he hadn't been eating either. That was a very good thing.

If she could take him off guard and just get the gun away, she had no doubt she could take him down. Twelve years of training would finally pay off.

When she sat she noticed her sister's ripped top. Her

bra was exposed, but other than that, she didn't look harmed. The other man however hadn't fared as well. His face was covered in garish plum-colored bruises and one of his eyes was swelling shut. "Did he touch you?" she murmured to her sister.

Maria shook her head, but Hope didn't miss the raw fear and sheen of tears in her eyes. Something *had* happened. Hope's gut dropped and rage took over. Deep-seated rage she hadn't known existed inside her. She wanted to claw and tear and rip his face apart for bringing any sort of pain to her sister.

She glanced over at Patrick. He wasn't even paying attention to them. With his head turned, he stared at the entrance. Probably looking to see if she'd brought backup. Talk about stupid. Well, she wasn't going to waste the only chance they might ever get.

"You son of a bitch." She lunged at him, taking him off guard. He turned, and their gazes collided before her body slammed into his. The gun flew out of his hand, but she didn't try to find it.

Through a haze she saw his eyes widen, but all she could focus on was his face. Her fist connected with his jaw, then it was all knees and fists. She pummeled him with whatever she could. He got in a few punches, but nothing fazed her. She felt absolutely invincible. Vague awareness of her head hitting something registered, but she latched onto his throat with her hands and wouldn't let go. Couldn't let go. Her nails dug in and—

"Stop it!" Maria's screams brought her back out of her fuzzy, violent reality.

She froze as she saw her sister. Hope's grip loosened and she stood. The man she'd feared for so long coughed and gasped from the floor. His tried to scoot away.

At first she thought he was scared of her, but when she heard the action of the slide chambering a round, she swiveled. Maria held the gun and she was pointing it right at Patrick. By her grip and stance, she obviously knew how to use it.

"Give me the gun, Maria. You don't want to do this." She went to stand by her sister.

Hope might not know much about her own flesh and blood, but something in her gut told her if Maria killed someone, she couldn't live with herself.

"No." Maria's hand wavered.

"Come on. You don't want to do this." She put a light hand on Maria's shoulder.

Maria didn't glance her way, but her voice shook and a few tears slipped down her cheeks. "He told me what he did to you...what he was going to do to both of us. He...he wanted you to watch."

Acid swirled in Hope's stomach. Maybe she should just let Maria kill him, but she couldn't. "This is my battle. Not yours. Now give me the gun."

Maria's hand wavered again. Hope let out a breath she hadn't realized she'd been holding when Maria handed it to her. Without a pause, she trained the gun on him where he still lay on the ground. His red-rimmed eyes shifted back and forth between the two of them, nearly bulging out of their sockets. He looked like some sort of maniacal cartoon character.

Hope wanted to shoot him. Something deep inside her wanted it so bad she was almost overcome with the urge to empty the entire chamber into his chest, but she couldn't. "Is your friend okay?"

Out of the corner of her eye, Hope watched Maria bend and check on the other man. "He's unconscious, but his breathing is steady."

"Good. Take my cell phone out of my pocket and call Luke."

Suddenly the boat shifted and they both glanced at each other. It could just be a shift of the water caused by boats coming into and leaving the marina. Hope wasn't taking the chance though. She pointed her gun toward the stairs leading up to the small entrance.

Her heart pounded erratically when she heard someone undo the latch to the entrance of the interior cabin. When familiar legs descended, she let her breath out, but not her guard down.

Luke swept the room, his gun drawn, before training it on Patrick's head. "Are you two okay?" His gaze switched between Hope and Maria.

Hope tucked the gun in the back of her jeans and nodded. Talking to Luke or getting a lecture on her rash behavior was more than she could deal with right now.

"Come on," she said to Maria. "We're going outside." She turned to Luke. "Can you stay with him?" She didn't wait for his response before taking Maria's hand. They brushed past Luke and up the small set of stairs. Let him deal with the monster in the cabin. Sirens sounded in the distance, and Maria clutched Hope's hand tighter. Silently, they half-sat, half-leaned against the inside of the boat deck.

Maria finally broke the silence. "I'm sorry."

"For what?"

She spread her hands wide, and her voice cracked. "For all this."

Hope shook her head. "You didn't do this. He did."

"But if it wasn't for me—"

"No, if it wasn't for *me*, you wouldn't have been involved in the first place." Guilt, relief and terror churned in her gut. The only blame lie at the feet of the monster in that cabin.

Maria didn't respond. She laid her head on Hope's shoulder and it took a few moments for Hope to realize the wetness on her arm was Maria's tears. Hope knew they were the same age, but in that instant she felt a thousand years older. Wrapping her arm around her sister's shoulders, she held her close.

What would happen now? She knew there would be hours of questioning at the police station and she didn't know how much she was willing to talk about. Not to mention there might be a trial of some sort. The Feds would be happy to have that monster in custody. Of that she was sure. Even if they couldn't get any of their charges to stick, at least they'd be able to get him on kidnapping.

Hope nudged Maria when she saw three men running down the dock toward them. Two were wearing police uniforms, but one was in plainclothes. All three jumped onto the boat, weapons drawn.

"In there." Hope pointed.

Two of the men nodded and entered the companionway. The man not in uniform sheathed his weapon and pulled out a notepad. Immediately he started firing questions at them, wanting to know why a man being pursued by the Feds had kidnapped them.

Hope was surprised by how fast they were working. Talk about interagency support. She was also surprised when Maria sat up, tears gone, and answered, "I have no idea, but we want medical attention for our friend," she pointed toward the cabin, "and to see our mother before we answer any questions. We're the victims here."

The man's eyes widened and he cleared his throat. "Of course, ma'am. The medic is on the way, but the Feds are gonna want to talk to you."

About four boats down, Sonja and Mac were struggling to get through a throng of policemen. Over a dozen men in uniform milled around the area, sectioning off everyone and refusing to let anyone in or out of the taped off area. Hope could see them, but didn't have the energy to wave. They'd be here soon enough, anyway. She wasn't sure what Mac was doing there so quickly though. She guessed Sonja had called him, but maybe she'd never know. Their recent bond was unsettling on too many levels, so Hope pushed the thoughts away.

The boat shifted again as two uniformed officers, Luke, and Patrick Taylor ascended the interior stairs. Patrick cast them a brief, venomous look, before one of the officers shoved him and ordered him to keep moving. At the same time, two paramedics hurried on to the boat.

"That way." Luke pointed to the newcomers.

The two men disappeared below deck and Luke immediately came to talk to Hope and Maria. "We're all going to have to head downtown and answer questions, but they agreed to let me drive us. They're giving us an escort, but you don't have to drive with them." He directed everything toward Hope.

"How did you find us so quickly?" she asked.

"I put tracking devices in all your shoes."

His words were said simply and with no apology. Spoken as if he'd just told her the time of day.

"You really are a piece of work," she muttered.

Maria tried to talk. "Hope, he—"

"Stop, please, just stop." Hope cut her sister off by waving a hand in the air. She didn't want any excuses. She didn't care about what he'd done. She cared that he didn't trust her enough to be straight with her. For the tiniest moment the night before, she'd thought they might be able to have some kind of relationship. She snorted at the thought, earning a strange look from her sister.

"Let's get out of here." Luke held out a hand for Hope.

She ignored it and linked arms with her sister instead. Maria raised her eyebrows at Luke, but didn't make another comment.

The flash of pain in his eyes almost made Hope feel guilty, but she shoved it away. Right now, her body needed to decompress. Years of wondering and suffering were finally over. And she had no clue how to handle her internal emotions. Add that to the fact that the man she was pretty sure she loved kept lying to her and her brain was about to go into overdrive.

Two men in uniform helped them up from the sailboat and stood on either side of her and Maria as they walked down the dock.

"We'll be escorting you to the station," the man next to her said.

She opened her mouth to respond, when a loud boom erupted. Like a bus backfire, except that it echoed across the water. Before she could think of what to do, Luke's heavy body covered both her and Maria, forcing them to the ground.

Her knees stung from the sudden impact against the wood, but she didn't care. She guessed what they'd just heard was gunfire. Shouting ensued from all directions, but Luke kept his hands over their heads and his body in place. Like a shield. She was also aware of the two policemen covering their position with their bodies, but she kept her head down.

There wasn't any more gunfire. That could mean any number of things.

"What's going on?" Maria shouted over the chaos.

"That was a gunshot." Luke's answer confirmed Hope's fears.

After a minute, one of the officers jostled the three of them, forcing them to raise their heads. He spoke into his radio, then spoke to them. "Someone shot the man we had in custody. Whoever it is, it doesn't look like they're after anyone else, but we need to get the hell out of here, *now*."

They all stood and sprinted for the parking lot. The time to ask questions would be later. In the ensuing mess, Hope didn't see Sonja or Mac. She just prayed Mac had nothing to do with any of this.

When they made it to Luke's truck, no one was waiting for them. Hope knew she'd seen her mother with Mac earlier. Where were they? Panic threatened to well up again. What if something had happened to them?

"Where's Sonja? I thought she'd be with you."

Luke shook his head and fired up the engine. "She sent me a text. She and Mac couldn't get through the police line so they're meeting us down at the station. They're probably already there."

Hope didn't respond. Instead she looked out the window. Police cars flanked every side of them. The blaring sirens should have drowned out her thoughts, but nothing could do that.

She gnawed on her bottom lip. If Mac had done something stupid, she prayed he didn't get caught. Because if he had killed Patrick Taylor, she sure as hell wasn't sorry the monster was dead. The only thing she couldn't live with was if Mac went to jail in an effort to protect her.

* * * * *

Hope turned up the volume to her iPod and sank deeper into the tub. After seven hours of filling out forms and answering the same questions twenty different ways, she could finally relax. Everyone was at the Santiagos' house, including Mac. Hell, even Jose was on his way back. Sonja was preparing enchiladas, but had told Hope to take her time getting ready.

That was exactly what she was doing. She definitely wasn't staying in the room they'd put her in before. The police wanted to blame the spray paint and break in on Patrick, but since he was dead, they'd never have the answers they wanted. The cops were too busy trying to figure out who had killed their suspect with one shot and gotten away from a crowded marina completely unseen.

That kind of maneuvering took some serious skill. A serious sniper with perfect accuracy.

At least the house was secure. Luke had upped the security three-fold, and with Mac there, Hope wasn't too worried. The massaging jets of the tub and soothing scent of vanilla was enough to make her fall asleep, so she pulled the drain plug and got out. Drowning wasn't on her agenda today. After changing into comfortable yoga-style pants and a pullover sweatshirt, she went in search of Luke. She wanted to talk to him before facing everyone else.

Luke had been trying to get her alone ever since returning to the house, but she'd managed to avoid him.

Even though she was in an upstairs bedroom, he'd stayed in the same room as before, probably because he knew she needed space. After walking down the stairs, she knocked once on his door, but secretly hoped he wouldn't be there.

No such luck. It opened seconds later.

"Hey. Can we talk?" The words came out in a rush.

He nodded and stepped back, letting her in. She had a sense of déjà vu from the night before, but ignored the memories. At least he was wearing clothes tonight.

Breaking things off with him was the easiest thing to do. She had to do it now before she fell too hard for him. Well, harder than she already had.

"I'm glad you stopped by. I wanted to apologize and explain what I did." He reached out to touch her arm, but she moved out of his reach.

If he touched her, she'd lose her train of thought and purpose. "I understand why you did it."

He let out a huge sigh. "You do? From the way you acted earlier, I thought—"

She cut him off. "I said I understood *why*, what I don't understand is why you didn't tell me. Did you think I'd be adverse to actions taken for *my* safety?"

"I didn't want to take the chance you'd say no. I'm so used to Maria, and—"

"I'm not her. Something you should know by now. She's stubborn just to be stubborn. This isn't about her, though. It's about you, and the way you view me."

"Hope, I couldn't stand the thought of anything happening to you." He shoved his hands in his jeans pockets.

She wanted to reach out and touch him. Anything to take away that pained look in his dark eyes. But she didn't. If she did, she'd crumble and wouldn't be able to finish what she needed to say. "I know we'll be involved in each other's lives from now on. It's inevitable. You provide their security and Sonja told me your parents are coming to visit next month so I assume you'll be here, too." Hope was leaving in the morning. Sonja and Maria were going to visit in a week or two and she planned to come back in a month to meet some of their friends. They were going to take her immersion into their lives a lot slower.

For the time being, she couldn't be in Miami another day. Too much had happened and she didn't exactly feel safe. More than anything, she missed her home, her friends, her small condo. She even missed Frank's cooking.

"What are you saying?" His Adam's apple bobbed up and down.

"I want things to end on good terms with us. If we're going to see each other occasionally, I don't want…awkwardness." In her heart she knew there might always be a little discomfort between them, but they were both adults. They could handle it.

"So you want to pretend nothing ever happened between us?" His words came out as a growl.

"I'm not saying that. Not exactly…jeez Luke, you never once mentioned your suspicions about my identity, you *stole* my DNA, and then you planted tracking devices in my shoes! I don't trust you, plain and simple. I don't know another way to say it. This could never work between us. Our relationship is too unbalanced with no trust. Maybe if you had asked me about at least one of those things, I'd feel differently right now. I like that you're protective of me but I don't want to be viewed as someone you think needs protecting all the time. I'm capable of making smart decisions. If you'd told me about the tracking devices I think I would have been okay with it—now we'll never know." She threw her hands up in the air, unsure how to continue. She didn't do relationships well and was unaccustomed to fighting or breaking up with anyone. This whole situation made her entire body tense.

"I don't know what to say. I am sorry." He stared at her with that dark, penetrating gaze, but she had no clue what he was thinking. Maybe he was relieved she'd ended it. She shifted from one foot to the other, waiting for more of a response that never came.

He was sorry but was that it?

Finally, she left.

He didn't try to stop her.

That's a good thing, she told herself. So why did she feel so lousy he hadn't even fought for her?

* * * * *

Luke rubbed a hand over his face as he sat on the edge of the bed. Everything Hope said was true. He couldn't defend himself. Hell, he didn't want to. He just wanted to take her in his arms and refuse to let her go. Yeah, he was sure that would go over real well.

What he'd done had been a little underhanded, but what if she'd said no? His gut roiled at the thought. Thankfully she'd been able to defend herself—quite capably judging from the way Taylor had looked before he'd been killed—but what if she hadn't, and he hadn't had a way to get to her?

The risk of losing her again was worse than the risk of her hating him. At least she was alive. The sad part was, he'd do things exactly the same way if given the opportunity. Right or wrong, he didn't know. The only thing he knew was Hope was alive and safe.

That's all that mattered.

The buzzing of his phone on the nightstand broke him out of his thoughts. Sighing, he retrieved it. When he saw the number, he flipped open his cell immediately. "Tell me you have good news."

"I don't know what I've got. All of the fingerprints from the room are from family members or employees." His friend Morgan had done him a huge favor and pushed their break-in case to the front of the line.

Disappointment sat in his gut like a lead weight. "Shit," he muttered.

"Not so fast. Jonas Ramirez's fingerprints were also in the room. I thought it was odd since he's the—"

"Gardener." Luke finished for him. His thoughts were already kicking into overdrive. Jonas had no business being in the house. Not that any of his guys would blink twice if he was. The man had been with the family for over four decades. Hell, he was practically invisible.

"Thanks for the info. I'll call you back." He disconnected before he received a response.

Jonas Ramirez had been with the family long before the girls had been born. If Luke remembered correctly, he was set to retire next month. He sprinted up the stairs and knocked once on Maria's door before opening.

"God, Luke! Wait for a response!" Maria looked over from the mirror where she was applying mascara.

Something had been bothering him for days and he

had to figure it out before confronting Jonas. He shut the door behind him and opened Maria's closet.

"Maria, why are these shoes covered in dirt and clay?" He picked up a ratty pair of tennis shoes. Maria worked out at the gym and she would never leave the house wearing something like this. It wasn't her style.

"None of your business," she snapped. Like lightning, she was across the room, snatching the shoes away.

"This is me you're talking to. What the hell is going on? I know I'm not crazy. The other day when I told you about the security system being disabled at the greenhouse, you looked guilty about something."

Her jaw clenched and for a second he thought she was going to tell him to pound sand, but she took a seat on the edge of her bed. The shoes dropped, spreading dirt particles all over the cream-colored carpet. She didn't seem to notice or care. When her pale blue eyes met his, a knife twisted in his stomach. If she'd had anything to do with Hope's harassment, all his belief in humanity was gone.

"The first couple times we met in the greenhouse I ruined two pairs of satin Manolo's so I started wearing those God-awful tennis shoes. I found them in Lydia's cleaning closet. We've been so careful. Every time we leave we reset the alarm, but maybe I forgot. Last time we were in such a rush, maybe I..." Her voice cracked, but she continued. "If it was me who forgot to set the alarm, it was an accident, I swear. I'll never forgive myself if I did."

Now she wasn't making any sense. "What are you talking about?"

"Isn't that what you're asking about?" Her eyes widened and tears threatened to spill over.

He ignored her question. "Who's 'we' and why have you been using the greenhouse?"

Splashes of red flared across her cheeks. "Kyle and I have been using the greenhouse to…you know. Not a lot, just a few times. Usually we meet at his place, but sometimes, we can't wait so…oh my God, I can't believe I'm telling you this."

Luke wouldn't have thought it possible, but her face turned an even darker shade of crimson. She groaned and covered her face with both hands.

"This is so embarrassing," she mumbled.

It was as if someone had poured a bucket of ice over him. "You and Kyle are seeing each other? Kyle, as in Kyle Vargas, my partner?"

She nodded, looking absolutely miserable. "Please don't tell anyone."

That's why she'd been using the greenhouse? He wasn't sure if he should be relieved or horrified. He shook his head and chuckled. "I'll talk to you about this later. Try and stay out of trouble for the next hour."

She tossed a throw pillow at him as he left the room. Kyle and Maria? He couldn't believe it. Shaking his head, he descended the stairs. Now that Maria was definitely off his list of suspects, he hated what he had to do.

If he was right, a lifelong employee had caused unspeakable pain and anguish to people he considered family. If he was wrong, he was accusing a sixty-year-old man of a horrendous crime.

"Marcus, have you seen Jonas?" Luke found Marcus in the kitchen drinking coffee with Mac. He kept his question nonchalant, not wanting to alert anyone.

Marcus shook his head and shrugged. "Try the greenhouse. I thought I saw a light on."

Luke glanced at his watch. It was after eight. Too late to still be working.

"Is everything all right?" Mac asked.

Luke nodded. "Fine…hey, any more news on who

shot Patrick Taylor?" He tried to keep his question casual, but doubted Mac was fooled.

"No. The police have no leads, but I doubt they'll be keeping me updated. I didn't even know the guy." The other man didn't flinch at the question, but in his gut Luke knew Mac had been behind it. Just as sure as he knew the sun would rise in the morning, he knew without a doubt Mac had hired someone. Probably an old Navy buddy.

Taylor had died on impact. One shot to the head and he'd gone down. The forensics gauged the shot had come from about seven hundred yards. It certainly wasn't impossible—the best snipers in the world could take someone out at two thousand plus yards—but it was still impressive considering the man had been surrounded by people.

Luke would bet a year's salary Mac had hired someone. If Mac hadn't been with Sonja the whole time, he might have been a suspect. Not that Luke cared who had done it. He couldn't prove it, and even if he could, he wouldn't. He sure as hell wasn't sorry that bastard was dead.

"Where is everyone?"

Both men nodded toward the direction of the back of the house. "Out on the lanai. Sonja cooked enchiladas. Better hurry before they're all gone," Marcus said.

Luke grunted and exited the kitchen. He knew Marcus had been in the Navy so maybe that's why he and Mac were talking. The other man's presence shouldn't bother him, but it did. It didn't take Freud for him to figure out why. Mac was the reigning male force in Hope's life, and though Luke wouldn't admit it aloud, he hated that. Childish? Probably. He just didn't care.

After saying hello to the women, he continued his trek across the expansive yard. Sure enough, a dim light shone through the glass.

"Anyone here?" he shouted upon entry. He also pulled his gun out. If Jonas was behind the destruction to Hope's room, he couldn't afford to take a chance.

"I'm in the back," Jonas's shaky voice called out.

Flowers and plant leaves brushed Luke's arms as he walked down one of the aisles. Seconds later, he found Jonas bent over a pot, clipping green leaves off some sort of plant. The man looked up when he heard him approach, and his eyes widened when he saw the gun.

"Is everything all right?" Jonas glanced around, his eyes darting nervously at anywhere but Luke.

"You tell me." Luke's voice was a sharp razor's edge. He hated doing this. Hated doubting someone he'd known for years.

"How did you know?" His voice was barely above a whisper.

Shit. There was his answer. It was like someone punched him in the gut. "I didn't until just now."

Jonas wiped his gnarled, dirty hands on equally filthy cargo-style pants.

"Why'd you do it?" Luke sheathed his gun. The only weapon the old man had was clippers but he wasn't fast enough to do any damage even if he wanted to.

Jonas leaned against his work table, then collapsed onto a rickety wooden stool. The small seat creaked under his weight. "It wasn't supposed to happen the way it did." He sighed and held his face in his hands, streaking himself with dirt.

"What was supposed to happen?"

Jonas looked up, his dark eyes wet with unshed tears. "Sherri and I took her. It was only supposed to be for a couple days. They'd pay the ransom and then we'd be rich. Simple." He coughed and wiped away a few stray tears. "But Sherri left. I always knew she wanted kids, but I never thought…" His voice trailed off and Luke guessed the older man was barely aware of his existence.

"Who the hell is Sherri? Did she work with you?" Luke had been a kid himself back when Hope had been taken, but he didn't remember anyone by that name working for the Santiagos'.

The older man's eyes focused on him. "She didn't work with me, she was my fiancé. That money was going to set us up for life. We'd always talked about sailing around the world. I never wanted kids and I thought she'd get over..." He trailed off again as he focused on the ground.

Luke didn't respond. It was hard to have any sort of empathy for a man who'd stolen an innocent little girl. Ripped her from her family and nearly torn them apart in their grief.

"What happens now?" he asked.

"That's not for me to decide." Luke motioned with his hand for Jonas to stand. He really hoped the old man didn't try to run. For now, he'd take him down to the police station. Luke had no clue what the statute of limitations was for kidnapping, if there even was one. Especially for a crime that had happened out of the country. Maybe they'd extradite him. Either way, it wasn't going to be Luke's problem. The court system could decide Jonas's fate.

Jonas stood on shaky legs. "I can't go to jail...I'm too old."

Luke took him by the arm, but the man fell to his knees. "Come on. I don't have time for this."

Jonas's face had turned a muted gray. Under the dim light, he looked as if death was staring him in the face. Maybe it was. He clutched his chest and gasped for breath.

"Aww shit, not now." Luke pulled out his phone and radioed Marcus. "I think Jonas is having a heart attack. Call 911."

Jonas gasped a few more times, then fell back into

the dirt. Luke checked his vitals and pounded on his chest. After a few minutes, Jonas sucked in a deep, strong breath.

"You're not getting away that easily," Luke muttered.

Jonas didn't respond. He laid his head back on the dirt floor and closed his eyes.　But at least he was breathing.

When the ambulance took Jonas away, Luke held his tongue. He'd already called the police and they were going to post a guard outside Jonas's hospital room. Luke would tell Sonja in the morning and let her decide what to do with the knowledge of Jonas's betrayal. Hope had had enough happen to her in the past week to last a lifetime. He didn't want to put a damper on her spirits now.

Any more bad news could wait until later. Much later.

It wasn't as if the old man was going anywhere.

Chapter 15

Hope slipped a summer dress over her head and quickly slid on a pair of sandals. She was supposed to meet Maria and Sonja for dinner, and Hope had come to learn how much her sister hated to be kept waiting. In Hope's opinion, Maria needed to learn to relax. A lot.

Maybe now that she was living in The Keys she would.

Hope still couldn't believe Maria had sold her half of her real estate business to her partner and was now living in the same building as Hope. If Maria stayed in real estate, Hope had no doubt Maria would be a success. The woman was a bulldog and she was already talking about opening up her own business here.

Even though Hope's life seemed to be heading back to normal—well, as normal as it ever would be with a whole new family to call her own—she hadn't quite learned to stop looking over her shoulder. It would come eventually, she knew that. Until then, every little noise at night startled her. That probably had something to do with the fact that she was sleeping alone when she could be sleeping with Luke. But she hadn't seen him in almost a month and he hadn't come after her. That alone

192

told her enough about his feelings. Even thinking about him shredded her insides to ribbons. She missed him so much. More than she'd imagined and more than she'd admit to anyone else. The short time they'd spent together had branded her in a way she didn't know that she'd ever get over.

The ring of her phone caused her to jump and scattered those painful thoughts. She fished her phone out of her purse and winced at her sister's name on the caller ID.

"Where are you? You're ten minutes late." Maria's voice held that note of annoyance Hope was coming to actually enjoy.

They might look alike on the outside, but they were like night and day. "I'm coming. Order me a glass of red wine and I'll be there in five minutes."

Maria snorted. "Five minutes in real time or in Hope time?"

Hope chuckled and locked her front door behind her. "Real time. I'm leaving right now."

Seconds later she walked down Duval Street, enjoying the salty air, but tripped and nearly stumbled into a drunk tourist when she saw a man who reminded her of Luke. Blinking a few times, she realized she was mistaken.

She clenched her fist against her purse strap. She had to stop doing that. Everywhere she went, she thought she saw him. It was maddening. She'd ended things, so she certainly shouldn't be conjuring him up in her mind. Unfortunately that's all she seemed to do lately. Think about Luke, dream about him, fantasize about what he could do with those talented hands and very sensuous mouth...She cursed her wayward thoughts.

When she entered her dad's Irish pub, it took a few moments for her eyes to adjust to the dim lighting. Maria had yet to eat there and had insisted they try it out. She glanced around, but the place was empty. Literally. Frank wasn't behind the bar, and there weren't any of his normal wait staff hanging around, pretending to work.

At one booth, a bottle of wine, candles, and two plates were laid out. She frowned as she stepped closer then pulled out her phone to call Maria when Luke stepped out from the kitchen entryway.

Her breath caught in her throat. She'd been aware of how much she missed him—she'd endured enough sleepless nights to prove it—but actually seeing him stole her very breath. Her legs threatened to give way as she stared into his charcoal gaze. "What are you doing here?" The question came out as a raspy whisper.

Luke stepped out of the shadows, looking lean, tired, and good enough to eat. "I had to see you."

While she mutely stared at him, he walked to the front door and locked it. At her raised eyebrows, he spoke again. "Frank let me have the place for the night. It's just us tonight."

"Frank did? So you guys are friends now?"

He shrugged and his lips curved into a half smile.

"Where are Maria and my mom?" Thinking of Sonja as her mother had happened quicker than she'd imagined.

"They're not coming," he said quietly as he studied her, gauging her reaction.

"So they were part of this?" Whatever 'this' was. Her heart stuttered rapidly as she drank in the delicious sight of him. Just looking at this man made every part of her flare to life. How the hell did I walk away from him?

He nodded and motioned toward the booth.

Unsure what to do or think, she took a seat. Immediately, he sat across from her and poured two glasses. Her throat clenched impossibly tight, but she managed to take a few sips. Anything to take off the edge of seeing Luke. Of being reminded of what she'd been missing for far too long.

"I've missed you." His honest words touched her core, releasing something wound tight inside her.

"Me too. A lot." No sense in lying.

"Last time we were together, you got to say what you wanted, but I never got to tell you how I felt." He looked at her for a long moment so she nodded.

"I'm listening."

He opened his mouth, but one of Frank's servers appeared with two salads. She picked up her fork and pushed lettuce around the plate just to keep her hands busy.

Luke placed both hands on the table, not bothering with the pretense of eating. "Everything you accused me of is true. Taking your DNA was wrong. It's not an excuse, but I couldn't stand to see Sonja go through any more heartbreak if you weren't Anna. I had to give her some sort of peace of mind. As far as putting the tracking devices in your shoes, I...I'd do it again under the same circumstances. Losing you wasn't an option, even if you hated me for it in the end. Knowing you like I do now, I wouldn't invade on your privacy like that. Not without your permission." His eyes held so much truth in them. As far as apologies went, his made her melt more than just a little.

"So what are you doing here exactly?" she asked softly.

"I want to take you out on a regular date." The corners of his mouth curved up into a slight smile. A hopeful smile.

She expelled a small breath. She'd been pining away after him for a month and he just wanted a date. "That's it?"

Those dark eyes of his glinted with unhidden lust. "Of course not. I want a whole lot more than that, but

I'm willing to settle for a date right now."

Hope bit her bottom lip. She'd missed him. A lot. She'd never had a serious relationship with a man, but she wasn't so stupid she didn't realize she loved him. They'd just done everything backward. They'd started with sex—albeit hot sex—and moved from there.

Silently, the server returned and removed their barely touched salads, before placing two steaming plates of Seafood Fontanella in front of them. She narrowed her eyes at him. "How did you know this was my favorite?"

Another slight grin as he picked up his fork. "I managed to get this much out of Mac."

Mac had known about this, too? She swallowed her surprise and took a bite.

"You still haven't answered my question."

"I don't remember you actually asking a question." She smothered a smile as she took a sip of wine.

"Okay, are you free this weekend?"

"The entire weekend?" Something told her he already knew the answer. If he'd managed to get Frank to agree to use the restaurant, he no doubt knew her schedule.

"Yes. I want you all to myself. No interruptions."

That sounded promising. "What did you have in mind?"

A wicked, almost mischievous smile. "You and me, doing stupid tourist stuff around town."

It sounded nice. Perfect, actually. And after so much time apart from him she knew without a doubt she wanted him in her life. Worry still niggled at the back of her mind. "How is this going to work? Us, I mean. Not for the weekend, but…" She didn't finish, mainly to hold on to some of her pride. What constituted his idea of long term? Her life had been tough and she dealt with that, but she wanted something normal for once. Marriage, maybe kids, but definitely marriage. She'd never thought about it before, but after she'd left Luke, she'd known she needed that kind of stability. And she wasn't so sure he was the kind of man who wanted all that.

He seemed to understand though. "Miami isn't far and I can work from anywhere."

"You can?"

Luke nodded. "As of a week ago, I'm no longer on full detail for the Santiagos' security. Kyle practically runs half the company anyway so now he'll be taking on more responsibility. Hell, I wouldn't be surprised if he bought me out in the next year."

"But…but, you love what you do." Or at least she assumed he did.

"I love you more."

His words sliced through her quickly fading barriers. She dropped her fork. The loud clatter was the only sound she could hear other than the rush of blood in her ears. "What did you just say?"

"I knew it that day at the restaurant, when you disappeared without telling us where you'd gone."

Her throat clenched as he reached out and grasped her hand in his. A shiver spread through her at the scorching touch she felt all the way to her toes.

"You don't have to say anything. I just wanted to lay all my cards on the table. No more lies or secrets between us."

"What if you get bored down here? The Keys are a lot slower than Miami and I don't plan on moving." Though she might consider it for him. The thought terrified her. "And I travel a lot." Sure, it was usually only for a week at a time, but she wanted him completely aware of her lifestyle.

He shook his head and expelled a long breath that sounded like laughter. "You can't scare me away Hope. I've already sold my condo…" He stopped, as if he realized he'd said too much.

Her heart leaped, wild and full of hope. "You did?"

Luke nodded and rubbed a hand over his face. "I didn't want to scare you, that's why I want to start out slow, but this is it for me. You're it for me."

How could things be so absolute for him? "You're sure? Just like that?"

"Yes. Just like that. I want it all from you. Till death do us part." His face was so solemn she knew he wasn't joking.

"I love you too." The words were out before she could think about stopping herself. She'd never told a man that before but at this moment she knew she needed to tell Luke. He had to know. No matter what happened between them in the future, they deserved a chance at happiness. And she couldn't be a coward any longer. Because that's what she'd been when she'd run from him and Miami.

He reached for her other hand and threaded his fingers through hers. "One day at a time."

She slightly frowned. "What?"

"We'll take this one day at a time. We know we love each other so everything else..." he shrugged, "will be a piece of cake."

She couldn't fight the smile spreading across her face. "Do you want to meet Maria and everyone after dinner?"

He nodded. "They're all at Mac's place. I told them if things went well, they could expect us in a couple hours. Unless of course you want to head back to your place instead..."

She mock kicked him under the table. "What happened to taking it slow?"

"We can take everything else except that slow. I've been going crazy without you in my bed." His voice had dropped to that incredibly sexy octave that made her toes curl and heat rush between her legs.

She was glad he'd been just as frustrated as her. In truth, she'd been missing him in her bed in more ways than one. When he was near, all her nightmares disappeared.

And he was right. One day at a time was all anyone could ask for. "Hmm, we'll see." But she knew they wouldn't make it to Mac's after dinner. She was hungry for Luke in a way that had her entire body humming with pent up desire and excitement. Going back to her place with him sounded like heaven.

Epilogue

One year later

Hope smoothed her hands down her simple white dress and stared at herself in the oval, full length mirror. She'd left her hair down and styled it into soft curls that fell around her face. She wore a veil and dangly diamond earrings—a gift from Luke's parents.

"You look gorgeous," Maria said behind her.

Hope swallowed hard and gave herself another critical glance. She'd opted for a simple white wedding dress. The silky material clung to her curves and fell right at her ankles in a soft, frothy swirl. Since it was strapless it showed off her tan—and she'd luckily been able to get rid of her tan lines before her and Luke's wedding. "You're sure?"

"You look like me, of course you're gorgeous." Maria grinned as she lightly fluffed Hope's veil. "It wouldn't matter what you looked like anyway. Luke is so smitten with you it's disgusting."

"You're one to talk," Hope murmured as she turned away from the mirror to face her sister.

To her surprise, Maria's cheeks tinged pink.

"Whatever. I don't think Kyle will ever work up the courage to propose to me… Or if he even wants to."

Hope bit back the words she desperately wanted to tell her sister. That Kyle had dragged Hope shopping to help pick out an engagement ring for Maria weeks ago. "I wouldn't be so sure about that."

Maria shook her head, her dark hair swishing around her face. "Whatever. Today is all about you and sister, you look stunning."

Hope grinned, but turned as the door to the room they were waiting in, opened. She'd opted to get married in a small Catholic church even though she wasn't religious. Luke didn't practice, but his family did. Plus Sonja and Maria were Catholic and it had seemed like such a small concession. One she definitely didn't mind making to keep the family in her life happy.

Sonja stepped inside and immediately batted away tears. "I swore I wouldn't cry and mess up my makeup," she said through sniffles. "You both look so beautiful. I love seeing the two of you together…"

Hope crossed the small distance and gathered her mom into a hug. She'd quickly gotten over her non-affectionate attitude once being inducted into the Santiago family. While Jose had never quite warmed to her, and Hope was pretty sure he and Sonja were headed for divorce—Maria had mentioned something a week ago—her mom and sister had run right over any issues she had with hugs and outward affection. Not to mention Luke's mom, her soon-to-be mother-in-law was huge on hugs and already pressuring her for a grandchild. While that could wait, Hope liked this new side to herself and loved having more people to call family.

Even Mac and Luke were on good terms. Luke was still a partner with Kyle, but he'd become more of a silent partner this past year. Now he and Mac were talking about opening up a restaurant together. And possibly a Jet Ski rental place. Whatever Luke decided to do, Hope just wanted him to be happy and this past year he'd been nothing but happy with her. They'd even closed on a house a month ago.

"If you start crying I will too and I refuse to look like a raccoon in the pictures." Maria's watery voice pulled Hope and their mom apart.

Sonja laughed lightly and ran her fingers under her eyes, catching the last few stray tears. "I'll be in the church. Your father is waiting right outside for you." After a quick peck on Hope's cheek, Sonja disappeared back through the door.

Hope knew Sonja mean Mac when she'd said 'your father'. There was also something about the way Sonja looked at Mac that made Hope wonder if something was going on between them.

Not a physical relationship because she knew her dad better than that—and Sonja for that matter—but if Sonja and Jose were getting divorced...Hope shook her head. It was none of her business. They were both adults and could do whatever they damn well pleased.

After the last year she'd had, nothing could faze her anymore. The man who'd stolen part of her childhood was dead—and that murder was likely to forever be unsolved. And the man who'd helped kidnap her as a child out of greed was also dead. Of a heart attack, weeks after his incarceration. That was fine with Hope.

Right now all she cared about was walking down that waiting aisle to the man she loved more than anything.

After a quick knock, one of Sonja's friends who'd helped organize most of the wedding popped her head in. "It's time."

Maria hurried out ahead of her and Hope followed to be met by Mac. His elbow was bent slightly as he waited for her to take his arm.

"You're beautiful," he murmured low enough for

only her to hear and she didn't miss the sheen of tears in his eyes.

If anything was going to make her well up, seeing Mac cry would do it. Swallowing hard she nodded tightly so she wouldn't break down.

As the doors to the church opened and she locked eyes with the man she loved with a fierceness that still moved her, she realized she'd never been happier than she was at that moment. They had their whole lives ahead of them to make millions of memories but this one day, this moment, would forever be seared into her brain.

Smiling, she gripped her dad's arm and began her walk toward the man she planned to spend the rest of her life with.

Dear Reader,

Thanks for reading Danger in Paradise! I really hope you enjoyed it. Often when I'm editing a book, words get cut and in some cases, entire scenes get the axe. In Danger in Paradise, I deleted the prologue because I realized it wasn't where the story should start, but I thought I'd share a little peek into this original scene for your enjoyment.

Happy reading,
Katie

Deleted Prologue from Danger in Paradise

12 years ago

Mac Jennings guided his sixty foot Wellcraft through the Atlantic, thankful for the calm seas. He hadn't caught any fish and all he wanted was to put his feet up and drink a cold beer. And if he was really lucky, maybe Anita would stop by after her shift at the hospital. Their relationship wasn't serious and never would be. But it was fun. He glanced at his watch and sped up when a dark shadow about twenty yards in front of his boat caught his attention.

"What the hell is that?" he mumbled. The moon and stars perfectly illuminated the coastal Florida water.

He'd been trolling these waters for years. Before he went to Vietnam and the many years since he'd been home. He knew where every inch of grass, reef, and pieces of sunken boat were located. His first thought was shark, but he wasn't near a reef and it was fairly shallow. Not prime feeding ground.

Mac kicked the boat into neutral and grabbed an oar he kept on board for emergencies. As the boat pulled up close, something painful tightened inside him. "Can you hear me?"

A young girl floated along with the tide, face up. Long dark hair pillowed around her face and body. Streams of crimson surrounded her small form in the calm seas. Reaching down, he plucked her from the ocean, surprised at how light she was. Her eyes were open and her chest moved, but she'd been badly injured.

"What's your name?"

No response, but at least her startling pale bluish gray eyes had awareness. When he moved, her eyes followed him. He grabbed a towel and wound it around her leg as tight as possible.

He rushed down to the cabin and laid her on one of the beds. She wasn't secure there, but he needed to get her to safety. She had two bullet wounds that he could see, one on her shoulder and another on her leg. For a split second he thought about calling the Coast Guard, but the girl was beautiful, young, and shot. The combinations could mean a whole mess of things and none of them were good.

The sex slave trade was unfortunately alive and well and he wasn't so naïve as to think such things couldn't happen in his country. If someone had dumped her to die, chances were they could just as easily pick up his transmission as the Coast Guard. And if they had more resources, they might reach him first. Not to mention, by the time anyone got here, he could have had her to the hospital already.

He returned to the top deck and revved the boat as fast as possible through the shallow water. He radioed his friend Frank who also happened to be a retired cop. "Frank, come in. Can you hear me?"

Static rustled briefly. "What's up man? You just finish up?"

He ignored the question. "Are you at the marina?"

"Yeah. Why?"

"Meet me at my slip in five minutes. Bring that extra set of keys to my jeep. And make sure the engine's running when I get there."

"What's going on?"

"See you in five. Out." He didn't have time to explain. The girl was maybe thirteen or fourteen years old and she'd lost a lot of blood. He guessed she was Cuban by her darker coloring, but her skin had paled considerably. Not a good sign.

Once he made it to the marina, Frank helped him stretch her into the back seat of the jeep. His only word was "shit", but beyond that he hadn't said anything else. Just as well. He didn't have answers. Frank drove and Mac sat in the back seat and put as much pressure on her wounds as he could.

Frank squealed to a stop in front of the emergency room doors and Mac jumped out. Anita stood at the information desk talking to one of the other nurses when she saw him. Immediately she sprung into action.

"My God Mac! What happened?"

"I found her floating not too far from the marina. She's been shot twice."

Anita started shouting orders like a drill sergeant and before he could blink, two men in green scrubs came and took her away on a gurney. Before Anita could follow he grabbed her arm. "Don't call the police yet."

"What?" She whirled on him, surprise in every line of her face.

"Just wait until she comes out of surgery. I've got a bad feeling about this. I'm not saying don't call them, I'm saying wait until she's awake. Did you see the dress she was wearing?"

Anita nodded. "Yeah, it probably cost more than I make in a year."

"Can you hold off calling?"

Her jaw clenched, but after a brief pause she nodded. "Done."

Eight hours later, Mac still sat by the young girl's bedside in the ICU. She'd come out of surgery two hours before, but he didn't want to leave her alone. Alone in a white sterile room that had the nauseating scent of a hospital. If she woke up by herself and panicked, he'd never forgive himself.

He, Frank and Anita were working on keeping the incident quiet for the time being. People in Key West liked their quiet lives and they didn't mind looking the other way if necessary. Locals looked out for each other and everyone on the mainland could be damned. If the locals could look the other way, he had friends in DC who owed him favors. A lot of them. He might not have to call one in, but his gut told him otherwise. When the girl woke up, he'd have his answers.

He nodded off, wasn't sure how long he'd been out when he was awakened by a hoarse voice. "Who the hell are you?"

He sat up and found himself staring into her unusual grayish blue eyes. Eyes that had seen too much. "I'm Mac. I found you."

He resisted the urge to shift under her intense scrutiny. "What happened?"

His head cocked to one side. "You tell me." When she didn't respond, he continued. "What's your name?"

She blinked but no response.

"Okay, what were you doing floating out in the middle of the Atlantic Ocean wearing a cocktail dress?" A dress that was much too sophisticated for someone her age. A telling sign in itself.

Just off the coast of Florida, the ocean was considered international waters. Wealthy 'business' men held parties and soirees on yachts and God only knew what went on out there. Everyone in The Keys knew about it but the government had their hands busy trying to stop the influx of cocaine into Miami from Cuba and South America. Unfortunately everything else took a back seat. An icy fist tightened around his heart at the thought of what she might have gone through.

Tears welled up and she glanced away.

Maybe a simple question would put her at ease. "How old are you?"

"Fifteen." Her voice was small in the quiet room.

He cleared his throat. "You were shot. Twice. We're supposed to contact the police in the case of—"

Her head swiveled back to face him and real, unabashed fear played across her pale, drawn, features. The first true sign of emotion he'd seen. "No! You can't, he'll find me."

"Who will find you?" Maybe this wasn't what he'd originally thought. She spoke perfect English, but she was still scared of someone.

She swallowed hard, the sound over pronounced in the small room. "Please don't call."

He tried one more angle. "Do you have any family? Is someone looking for you?"

She snorted, but her eyes darkened, belying a deep rooted sadness. "I have no one."

What was he getting himself into? He'd already lost a wife and daughter. He liked his life simple. How could he even think about helping some strange girl?

When he didn't respond, she pushed up and tugged at one of the IVs in her arm.

He started to stop her, but decided against making any quick movements or physically touching her. "Stop, we're not going to involve the police. Just sit back and rest." He rubbed a hand over his face. Turned out he was going to have to call in a couple favors after all.

"Do you promise?" She left the IV alone and settled back against the pillow, but he didn't miss the cautious gleam in her eyes.

"I promise." And he meant it.

With those two words, something flared in her eyes. And even though he didn't know her, something inside told him the emotion was foreign to her.

Hope.

ACKNOWLEDGMENTS

First I must thank my wonderful readers for their amazing support! And as always, I also owe a huge thank you to Kari Walker. I'm also incredibly grateful for the fantastic design work by Jaycee with Sweet 'N Spicy Designs. She's done many of my covers, including this one, and each time she outdoes herself. And as always, I'm thankful to God for so many wonderful opportunities.

Complete Booklist

Red Stone Security Series (romantic suspense)
No One to Trust
Danger Next Door
Fatal Deception
Miami, Mistletoe and Murder
His to Protect
Breaking Her Rules
Protecting His Witness

Individual Romantic Suspense Titles
Running From the Past
Everything to Lose
Dangerous Deception
Dangerous Secrets
Killer Secrets
Deadly Obsession
Danger in Paradise
His Secret Past

Deadly Ops Series
Targeted

Individual Paranormal Romance Titles
Destined Mate
Protector's Mate
A Jaguar's Kiss
Tempting the Jaguar
Enemy Mine
Heart of the Jaguar

Moon Shifter Series (paranormal romance)
Alpha Instinct
Lover's Instinct (novella)
Primal Possession
Mating Instinct
His Chosen Wolf (novella)
Avenger's Heat

About the Author

USA Today bestselling author Katie Reus fell in love with romance at a young age thanks to books she pilfered from her mom's stash. Years later she loves reading romance almost as much as she loves writing it. However, she didn't always know she wanted to be a writer. After changing majors many times, she finally graduated with a degree in psychology. Not long after that she discovered a new love. Writing. She now spends her days writing dark paranormal romance and sexy romantic suspense. For more information on Katie please visit her website at www.katiereus.com or her facebook page at www.facebook.com/katiereusauthor.

8002592R00118

Made in the USA
San Bernardino, CA
24 January 2014